AF291827

THE FOREVER MAN

BOOK FOUR: UNICORN

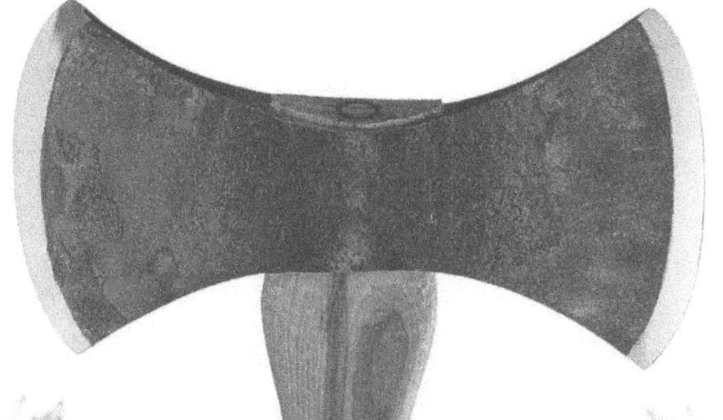

CRAIG ZERF

© 2014, Author Craig Zerf/C. Marten-Zerf Published by Anglo American Press

ALL RIGHTS RESERVED. This book contains material protected under International and Federal Copyright Laws and Treaties. Any unauthorized reprint or use of this material is prohibited. No part of this book may be reproduced or transmitted in any form or by any means, electronic or mechanical, including photocopying, recording, or by any information storage and retrieval system without express written permission from the author / publisher.

Once I said to a scarecrow, "You must be tired of standing in this lonely field."
And he said, "The joy of scaring is a deep and lasting one, and I never tire of it."
Said I, after a minute of thought, "It is true; for I too have known that joy."
Said he, "Only those who are stuffed with straw can know it."
Then I left him, not knowing whether he had complimented or belittled me.
Kahlil Gibran

CHAPTER 1

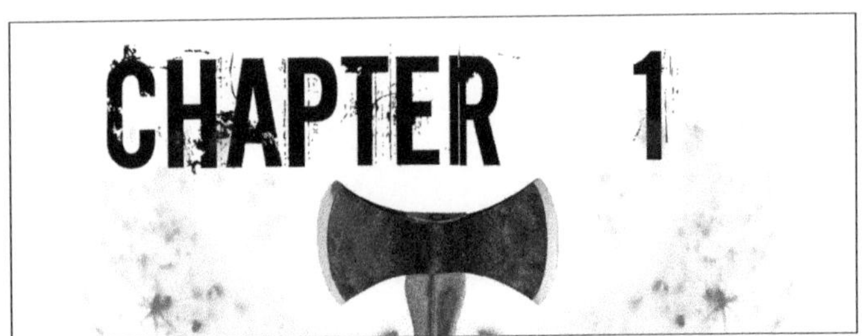

Swiftly it ran, muscular haunches bunching and coiling under its glossy white coat as it did. Breath steamed from its mouth and lather saturated its heaving flanks. But so fleet was its progress that naught could overhaul it.

The chittering of the enemy hunters sounded behind it and above, the sound of the whirring of chitinous wings from the legions of the smaller flying scouts.

Undaunted it gathered its remaining strength and thundered on, heading towards the source, its four hooves churning up the sod as it ran. Striving to reach the intersection of ley lines that crossed in the center of the stone circle. Because, for the first time in living memory, it could feel the beckon of the power-light and it could sense the open gateway between the now and the perpetuity of infinity.

With a last surge of beleaguered muscle, it galloped into the center of the circle. Lightning struck. The sky folded in on itself.

The circle was empty.

And in another time and place, in another circle, it appeared. Its chest heaved with exhaustion and its mighty legs trembled in near collapse, but once again, it had survived. It was the very last of its kind and had lived alone for years uncountable, but now its purpose had arrived.

Almost twice as large as a thoroughbred stallion. Its eyes were deepest green and behind them lurked an intelligence that could only be born of boundless life experience. And, as it flicked its mane from side to side, the single large horn on its head cut the air like a sword, reflecting the wan sunlight like a polished steel blade. Light glistened off its pure white hide that was marred only by a single black mark on its left flank. A mark the size of a man's palm.

Lemniscate.

The mark of infinity.

∞

The mark of the unicorn.

The mark of The Forever Man.

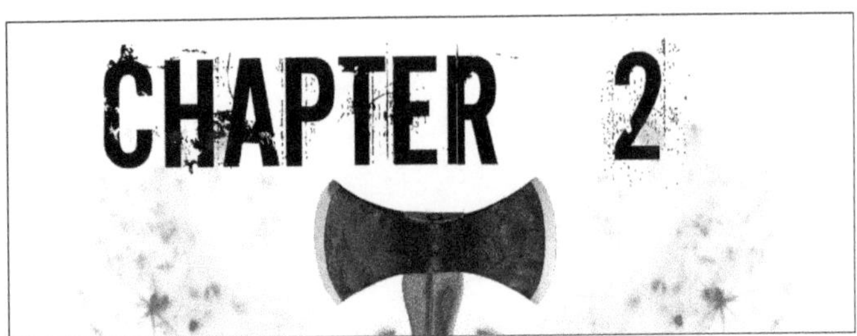

CHAPTER 2

Nathaniel beckoned to Tad, calling him over with a crook of his finger. The Marine's dwarven friend moved close, using the trees and bushes as cover, his movements stealthy. A craft built from years of clandestine operations and thousands of hours of outdoor hunting.

The Marine pointed at the group of heavily armed alien warriors that stood encamped about a hundred yards from the tree line.

'It's not a full battle group,' whispered Nathaniel. 'Probably twenty Orcs and thirty goblin archers. No humans on horseback and no Fair-Folk, by the look of it.'

Tad studied the group before he nodded his agreement.

'Still enough to cause us some serious problems,' he said. 'What do you reckon? Should we wait them out?'

Nathaniel glanced back into the forest. The thick trees and the vegetation hid a small train of four wagons and some twenty mixed beasts of burden. Horses, donkeys, and oxen.

He shook his head. 'They might be camped there for days. We have no water and it won't be long before one of our party will make some sort of noise that will give us away. After all, they're not pros. They're just farmers and tailors and stuff. The only way is for me to create some sort of serious diversion. Lead them away. Then you and the refugees split for the wall. I'll follow you after I've sorted something out.'

'No way,' disagreed the little big man. 'I'll create the diversion. We can't have the king of the Free State running around as live bait for an Orc battle group. That's insane. You shouldn't even be here. The only reason that you are, is because you're so pig-headed and stubborn that we can't seem to instill any sort of common sense into you. Some might even call you a moron.'

'Hey,' objected the Marine. 'Is that any way to address your king?'

'Whatever,' answered Tad. 'You can't go.'

'I can, actually,' said Nathaniel. 'And I will. And before you blow a big end, let me explain. Firstly, you simply aren't fast enough.'

'I'll take a horse.'

Nathaniel shook his head. 'We both know that won't work. They'll never even bother to attempt to chase a man on horseback. They know full well that they'll never catch him. No, the bait has to be on foot and it has to be fast enough to escape. That means me.'

Tad grasped the Marine by the shoulder, and looked into his eyes, his expression stern. Grim. 'It's not a game, my friend,' he said. 'Too many people depend on you. Be careful. I'm serious.'

Nathaniel grinned. 'Lighten up, Tad. We only live once.'

Tad grinned. 'No … I only live once. You live forever. But remember, we don't necessarily want to test that theory beyond a point. Not sure how you'd recover if one of those Orcs actually separated your head from your shoulders.'

'He'd have to catch me first,' quipped Nathaniel as he started to strip off for running. He removed his armor and his greaves and his tunic, leaving on only his kilt and a pair of light leather boots. He pulled a leather strap over his shoulder and stuck his axe through it so that it hung against his back. Finally, he tied a canvas water sack to his belt alongside a small leather pouch that contained his sling and a handful of lead slugs.

'I'm going to circle them,' he told Tad. 'No good coming at them from here. Could give away our position. I'll come at them from the East, slingshot a few of them, shout a few taunts and run like crazy. You know Orcs—no tactical nous at all, they'll all simply try to kill me. As soon as they start following me, count to sixty and then you guys move on out. Okay?'

Tad bumped fists with the Marine. 'Okay, my lord. Let's do this.'

Nathaniel grinned again and then slipped into the trees, disappearing almost immediately with his customary supernatural stealth.

The little big man did not have to wait long until Nathaniel appeared on the opposite side of the Orc encampment. The Marine stood in plain sight for a few seconds, calmly drew his sling from his pouch, loaded it with a lead slug, spun it around his head and fired.

The two-ounce lead projectile whipped across the intervening space and struck a goblin archer on his temple, dropping him like a pallet of faulty merchandise. He was dead before his body hit the ground. The next slug took an Orc in the neck, not penetrating the inch-thick skin but causing a squeal of porcine agony.

'Hey, pig-faces,' shouted Nathaniel as he let fly with another shot that bounced off the same Orc's skull, causing him to drop to one knee. 'Time to pay the piper.'

He turned and ran, and the battle group thundered after him.

'Time to pay the piper,' snorted Tad to himself as he counted off a minute. 'What the hell does that mean?' He shook his head, covering his concern with irritation. He turned to his flock. 'Come on, people,' he called. 'The king has given us a bit of breathing space, let's not dally. Follow me.'

Tad mounted up and led the wagon train out of the forest and north towards the Free State.

***

Nathaniel slowed down and waited for the Orcs and goblins to catch up. He had inadvertently outpaced the bulk of the battle group and it would do no good to outrun them to such an extent that they simply gave up the chase. He slung another lead slug and let fly as the first Orc became visible through the trees. The projectile struck the creature in the eye and it dropped to the turf, yipping and squealing as it tore at the wound with its claws. The Marine forced down any feeling of pity as he fired another slug at a goblin, shattering its shoulder and spinning it to its knees.

He turned and ran again.

Straight into one of the biggest Orcs that he had ever seen. Over six foot high and a solid three hundred pounds plus.

As a rule, all Orcs were very much the same size and build. About five foot ten inches and 250 pounds. Overlong arms, inch thick rubber-like skin, deep set eyes, no nose, no visible ears, and a thin slit for a mouth. The reason for this being that they were specifically created for battle. Over countless years the Fair-Folk had distilled their warriors into the essential properties that made up the battle Orc. And it was not only their physical attributes that were controlled. Likewise, their mental capacities were limited to following orders without question. They reacted to situations as opposed to preempting them. If they were threatened, they fought back. If the enemy ran, they chased. They would fight to the death without hesitation, and they would kill without remorse.

But what they would not do was tactically outflank an enemy and then ambush him.

Except—this one had.

The Orc punched Nathaniel in the chest. The blow picked the Marine up and threw him back for over ten feet. He winced as he struck the ground, breathing hard in an attempt to get his wind back.

As Nathaniel got to his feet the Orc was on him again, slamming lefts and rights into him with crushing strength. The Marine felt a rib break as the Orc punched him once again. If he had been any normal human then he would, in all probability, be dead by now.

But Nathaniel was not any normal human. In fact, he was about as abnormal as a human could be and still be classed as a human. He ignored the pain of his broken rib, knowing that, in a few minutes, it would be all healed up, and instead he concentrated on moving. He sidestepped fast and slammed a combination of punches into the Orc's abdomen. Then, without pause, he rolled on the ground, under the Orc's defenses and kicked him in the knee. The unexpected move dropped the Orc to the ground and Nathaniel punched him twice in the head. Both of them good solid blows, putting his whole bodyweight behind them.

He waited for the Orc to keel over. Instead the creature stood up, shook his head, and started forward again.

Nathaniel was amazed. And it suddenly struck him that the Orc had yet to draw his broadsword.

The Marine held up his hand. 'Hey,' he said. 'Why haven't you drawn your weapon?'

The Orc shrugged. 'Why haven't you drawn yours?' he countered.

Nathaniel said nothing.

'Come on,' urged the Orc. 'Let's finish this before the others arrive.' He stepped forward and threw a massive roundhouse punch at the Marine.

Nathaniel moved his head with the blow but did not deign to dodge. Then he bowled a right arm overhead blow back at the Orc, striking him flush on his forehead.

The Orc shook his head and punched back, smashing his massive paw into Nathaniel's mouth and bringing a welter of blood to the surface.

And so, the two of them stood, trading blows without thought or question of either tactics or reason. It was simply a test of brute strength. A test of courage. A physical test that had been broken down into its most primitive primeval form.

After six or seven blows each the Orc finally dropped to one knee. Nathaniel clubbed him on the temple with a huge right hook and the gray-skinned creature slid sideways to the floor.

The Orc made a final attempt to stand but found that he could not, so he simply lay on the floor and stared up at Nathaniel, his eyes a mixture of disbelief and respect.

The Marine stared back and then he drew his battle-axe from his shoulder-belt, swung it high in the air and brought it down on the Orcs neck … stopping the blade as it touched the alien's skin.

Then, with a flick of his wrists, he replaced the weapon, threw the Orc a salute and disappeared into the forest, this time running too fast to warrant any form of pursuit.

And Orc Sergeant Kob breathed a sigh of relief.

***

Nathaniel loped along at a pace a little slower than a normal human's full sprint. He was using up energy at a prodigious rate but didn't mind; as he knew that he would catch up with Tad and the refugees a little after nightfall. Then he could replenish his fluids, eat his full, and get a decent night's sleep.

As he ran he marveled at the changing landscape that lay all around him. Although it was now over twenty years since the first pulse had struck the Earth, driving mankind back to the Dark Ages, Nathaniel had only spent some four of those years in the present time. For twenty of the current years he had been magically transported to ancient times, where he had become king of the Picts and rallied the Pictish tribes to fight against the Roman invaders.

When he had left, the land had already started to change. Plants had begun to invade the towns and cities, animals like deer and badgers and rabbits had begun to proliferate in abundance and the cessation of global warming had, paradoxically, caused the summers to shorten and the winters to become longer and harsher.

As well as this, around 90 percent of the population had died. Over sixty million people. This had left most of the country empty and unpopulated.

But now, over twenty years on, much more radical changes had taken place. The winters had reduced the vast stretches of tarmacadam highways to degraded rubble. Grass grew in the cracks and moss covered the rest. The rotting husks of millions of vehicles lay discarded along the old routes. Stripped for whatever people could use and then left to slowly corrode away into hollow rotting husks.

The roofs of uninhabited houses had all collapsed allowing trees to grow in their interiors. Home gardens no longer existed as tree growth was unchecked by man's pruning and cutting.

Massive packs of feral dogs roamed the inner cities, sometimes interbreeding with the packs of wolves that were now ever-present. There were no longer specific breeds of dogs in the wild, only a homogenous blend of wolf and canine.

Birds of prey now claimed the crumbling skyscrapers as their eyries from which to hunt rodents and small game.

The more exotic animals that had survived release from the zoos now thrived. Prides of lion. Tigers. Herds of llamas. Bears. Hyena.

Most of the grasslands that were unkempt by humanity had reverted to forest and it was now easily possible to travel both the length and breadth of the island without ever leaving the shelter of the trees.

Humanity had adapted. They had overcome. But they had been driven to the very edge of extinction. And then the Fair-Folk had come and conquered. And Nathaniel saw them in the same light as he viewed the pulse. They were a danger to humanity that must be overcome. A disease. A pack of feral dogs. An enemy.

With that thought foremost in his mind, he crested a hill and saw signs of Tad and his refugees in the distance. He increased his speed to catch them up.

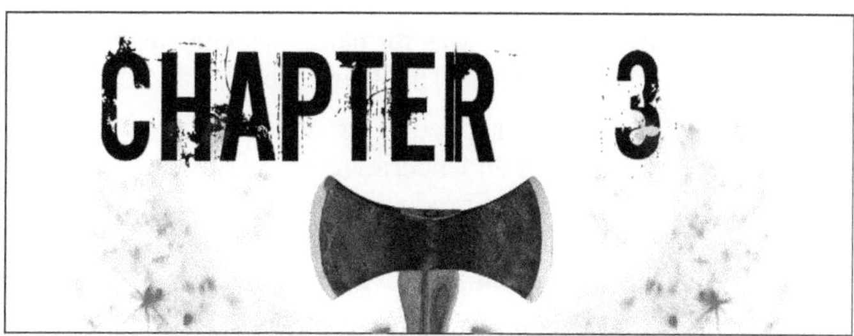

CHAPTER 3

They were two brothers. Twins. But not identical. Their names were Donny and Lonny Bonnyman, and that ludicrousness was one of their many hardships that they could not blame directly on the Fair-Folk.

The brothers had just turned sixteen. They had been orphans for almost nine weeks now, having lost their father some six months before and then their mother just over two weeks ago.

The twins had been born after the pulse and had only known life under the yolk of the Fair-Folk and their minions. But their father, who had been a university lecturer in the Classics, had spent much of his time teaching them. Both were fluent in Latin and ancient Greek as well as being extremely well versed in the history, culture, and thought of the civilizations of ancient Greece and Rome.

As well as having been a lecturer in the Classics during pre-pulse times, Professor Bonnyman had been a well-known activist, leading public revolt against the war in Iraq, the privatization of the National Health Service, and the channeling of government spending into the new Star Wars program as opposed to education.

When the Fair-Folk had first appeared and started taking control, he had approved. He thought of them as benevolent dictators. However, it was not long before he started to disagree. He changed his description to draconian and accused them of being harsh and overbearing in their rule. But he was careful never to flagrantly break any of their stringent rules with their harsh punishments. Instead, he skirted carefully along the border between actual dissent and barely tolerable disagreement.

So, instead of being punished in any outright fashion, the Fair-Folk decided instead to censure him. He was formally condemned and reduced to a new class that the aliens had created. That being the class of "Underman."

The class of Underman was applied to the whole family of the person that was initially sanctioned. As an Underman, one was banned from ownership of land or any means of production, be that tools or premises. Undermen were not allowed to fish nor hunt nor gather food. They could work at only the most menial of jobs and when paid were not allowed to eat meat or bread. They were allowed no access to healers, doctors, midwives, or apothecaries. And they were not allowed to own any weapons.

Being sanctioned and declared an Underman was, quite simply, a long and very slow death sentence.

The twins had poached game and fish in an effort to supply the family with enough protein to live but their father simply gave up and faded away. Slipping into unconsciousness and death in his sleep, his body a mere wasted vessel for his broken mind.

Their mother had lasted only a few more months, unable to live with both a broken heart and a broken spirit.

And now the twins seeked revenge.

They had collected over ten rats and had left their dead bodies tied up in a sack for over a week, allowing them to rot to a stage where liquid dripped from the sacking and maggots crawled over them like handfuls of living rice grains. Then, using skills brought from countless nights of illegal trapping and poaching, they had used the cover of darkness to sneak into the Orc's garrison. Their plan was simple. Drop the sack into the well, in the hope that they would poison the water supply and then run away. It was a simple plan and was bound, in some way, to at least inconvenience the Orcs. And, as Donny had said when he thought of it, it was only the first in a long line of disruptive acts that they were to embark on.

Lonny moved stealthily through the shadows. Behind him, Donny carried the dripping sack. The two of them crouched down behind a wagon and contemplated their next move. The well was in the center of an open area that was brightly lit with torches. On the periphery of the clearing stood an Orc guard.

'What now?' whispered Donny.

But before Lonny could answer there was the chilling sound of steel being drawn from leather. A silken sound that both boys knew was the precursor to a violent death.

'Turn around slowly, boys,' sighed a voice behind them. The words spoken so softly as to be almost a zephyr of wind, or the faint susurration of an insect's wings.

Both heads swiveled slowly to look.

In the shadows, only barely visible, was the faded outline of a male human being. His face was covered in dark mud and he wore clothes that were tied with lengths of sacking in which he had pushed leafy twigs and clumps of grass. The broken outline and natural coloring made him close to invisible in the darkness. Even the blade of the vicious knife that he had drawn had been blackened with soot, preventing any inadvertent reflection of light that may give away his position.

'What are you doing here?' the man whispered. Donny held up the stinking sack in reply.

'We could ask the same of you, sir,' answered Lonny in a shaking voice.

'You could,' agreed the man. 'Now answer me. And be quick before I gets irritable and decide to slit your throats.'

'We came to poison the well, sir,' continued Lonny. 'The sack is full of rotten rats.'

The man nodded slightly. 'Not bad. But you'll never get to the well without raising the alarm. Tell you what, boys. Set the sack down and follow me.'

The twins looked at each other and, with an unspoken agreement, concurred that they actually had little to no choice in the matter. The man slid into the darkness and the twins followed.

He led them to a building that was situated behind the main barracks. Two Orc guards stood outside the front entrance and a row of flickering torches lit the open area in front of the building. The man motioned the boys to get down and both of them prostrated themselves, still keeping to the shadows. Then the man opened the rucksack that he was carrying and started to clip together a small, two shot, crossbow. It was an ingenious affair. The butt constructed of laminated wood and the two sets of arms in stainless steel that looked as if they may have originally come from the leaf suspension of a car or truck.

Once the weapon was assembled he slotted two short steel bolts into the twin slots and, without warning, lined the bow up and pulled the triggers.

Both bolts slammed home with uncanny accuracy and both Orcs dropped noiselessly to the ground, a feathered steel bolt sticking from both of their right eye sockets.

The man sprang to his feet and ran across the open ground to the door of the building.

He looked back at the boys who were both riveted to the floor in shock.

'Come on,' he said. 'Help me.'

The twins sprang to their feet and followed him.

He eased the bolt open to the front door and slipped inside, closing the door as soon as the twins were in. Then he struck a flint and lit a small torch.

It was immediately apparent that they were in the main armory. Hundreds of long bows lined the walls and, at the far end, countless thousands of goose-fletched cloth yard arrows lay staked in oilcloth-wrapped bundles. Along the center of the warehouse, leaning together for support were pikes and broadswords and wooden steel-rimmed shields.

The man pulled three flasks from his rucksack and handed one to each of the twins, pulling the stoppers out as he did so. The pungent smell of fish oil filled the air.

'Come on then,' he said to the twins. 'Splash this over everything. Particularly the arrows and the bows. They'll burn the best.'

The boys scurried around the warehouse, liberally dousing the weapons with the stinking oil. The man finished his flask and pulled another one from his rucksack. He poured the contents all over the wooden shields in the middle of the room then he headed to the door.

'Let's go, boys,' he said. 'Unless you're big on self-immolation.'

The twins rushed after him and followed him through the opened door. With a last look over his shoulder the man chucked the flaming torch into the oil-soaked armory. There was a pause and then a low booming whoosh of conflagration as the oil took the flame.

The man grinned, his teeth shockingly white against his mud-smeared features.

'Now what?' asked Lonny.

'Now,' said the man. 'We run like hell. Follow me.' And he set off like a long dog after a rabbit.

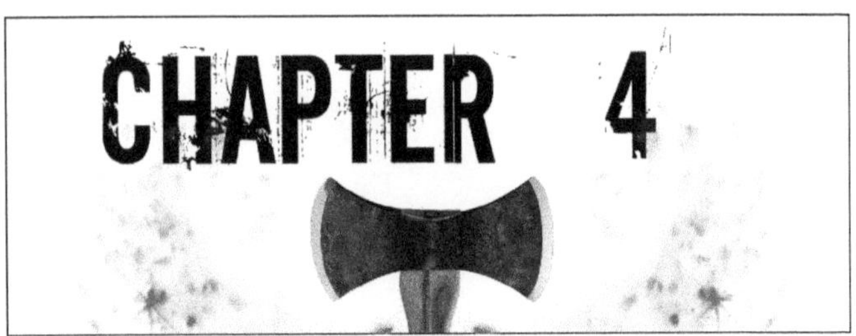

The massive gates slid to a close. They ran on railway tracks and old locomotive wheels, powered by a series of pulleys and gears that Roo, the resident genius, had designed and constructed. Normally gates were considered to be a weak point in a defensive wall, however, these gates were so massive and so thick that they were easily as strong as, if not more so, than the stone wall itself.

The wagon train rolled onwards as they followed Tad and Nathaniel into the heart of the main wall fort. The entrance to the Scottish Free State.

Nathaniel steered his horse to the stables, leaving Tad to take care of the new refugees as he looked forward to a bath and a hot meal. He hoped that he would have a little alone time before he was inundated with requests for his attention. He had managed to build a substantial buffer between himself and the day-to-day running of the kingdom, but it still seemed that every minor decision needed his attention. Everything from new tax levels, to grain quotas, to educational needs for children, landed up on his desk.

He longed for the times when he was still but a Marine Master Sergeant. High enough in the military structure to be above the pile of crap that officers sent running downhill but low enough to avoid any really serious decisions apart from the day-to-day combat ones.

Roo wanted permission to strike a new range of coins, arguing that the simple copper, silver, and gold range did not allow for enough diversity. Tad argued that they had more important things to concentrate on, like land rights for new refugees and startup capital for all that arrived in the Free State. Gogo was insistent that the teaching of magik control to gifted children should be the Free State's main priority and that they should be spending more time seeking out any and all gifted children to enroll in a college of magiks.

The newly appointed General, Mister Ronald Carson, ex pre-pulse British army general and professional soldier, whom Nathaniel had recently promoted to head of the Free State army, was insistent that all available time and effort should be spent on preparing for an inevitable war against the massed forces of the Fair-Folk.

And the most exhausting thing about the whole melting pot of ideas was … they were all correct. Every point seemed to be just as important as the next. It gave The Forever Man a headache just thinking about it. Therefore he tried, whenever possible, to escape to the field to simplify his life back to the days when decisions were based on the principles of combat and tactics as opposed to games of thrones and the painful politics of a burgeoning nation.

He dismounted and handed the reins of his horse to a stable boy. Then he made his way back to his residence.

Although Nathaniel was king of the Free State, his living quarters were very simple. A low, sprawling affair that was half stone and mortar and half canvas and wood. If he needed another room for meetings or administration staff he simply asked Roo to tack another one on, and so the royal "palace" was more tent city than regal building. And that was how Nathaniel preferred it to be. For, although he was king, in the deep recesses of his mind, he would never be more than a Marine Master Sergeant. And proud of it.

The Marine pushed open the unlocked front door to his residence and the smell of fresh baked cherry pie immediately assailed his nostrils and started his mouth watering. But at the same time his heart dropped.

There was only one person that he knew that baked cherry pie and that was Milly.

Nathaniel had first met her as a young girl, saving her from a group of thugs after her family had been beaten to death in front of her. She was seven years old and he had taken care of her until she was nine. Then he had left her in the care of Gramma Higgins and her two grown daughters. He had left her so that he could continue with his quest. The geas that had been imposed on him, compelling him to continue north at all costs.

But then the Marine had been magically taken to the time of the Picts and when he had returned, over twenty years had passed. During this time Milly had been kidnapped and brutally gang-raped. She had grown up hating Nathaniel and blaming him for the hardships and cruelties that had befallen her after he had left.

He later met up with her when she had become a worthy human, a reward class of human bestowed on people who were fanatically loyal to the Fair-Folk and their minions. She had professed both her hatred and her undying love for the Marine. Seeing him as her only real savior and protector. But Nathaniel could not get over their age gap. To him she was still a nine- or ten-year-old girl. Only two years had passed since he had last seen her, and he could not rationalize the little girl he knew with the grown, sexually active woman that she now was. He did truly love her and his guilt at having left her was immense, but he could think of her only as a child. A daughter. Never a lover.

So, once again, he had left her, and in revenge, Milly had convinced the Fair-Folk leadership to attack the Free State in order to kill Nathaniel. But, on realizing what she had done, she had ridden to warn him, and since the Free State's victory over the Fair-Folk attack, she had stayed with the Free State and had spent all the time that she could trying to convince Nathaniel that she was now a full-grown woman capable of receiving proper adult love from him.

Nathaniel had done his best to explain and to kindly rebuff her advances, but it had proved difficult, as she was highly strung, and her life was governed almost entirely by her feelings of lost love and rejection.

She came running down the corridor towards him, her dark hair pulled back into a ponytail, dressed in a short, clinging green cotton dress, her feet bare and her long, strong limbs exposed. A small streak of white flour on her face. Domesticated war paint.

'The watch told me that you were near,' she said. 'So, I put the cherry pie in the oven so that it would be ready when you got here.'

She threw her arms around the Marine and tried to kiss him on the lips. But Nathaniel turned his head slightly to direct the kiss onto his cheek. Milly said nothing, but her eyes narrowed at her obvious displeasure.

She took his hand and led him to the kitchen. 'Come,' she said. 'I have ale and roast venison with potato. Eat, and then I shall run a bath for you and scrub your back.'

Nathaniel laughed awkwardly. 'No need for that, Milly,' he said. 'I've been washing myself for over thirty years, I'm sure that I can continue doing so for the foreseeable future.'

Milly raised an eyebrow. 'We'll see,' she said.

Nathaniel ignored her and sat down to eat. No sooner had he taken his first mouthful when there was a knock on the door.

'Could you see who that is?' he asked Milly.

She shook her head. 'Ignore them. This is our time. That's the problem with us, don't you see?' she continued. 'We never get any time alone. How can a relationship ever work if we're never alone?'

'Milly,' replied Nathaniel. 'That's not the sort of relationship that we have. And you know that. I love you, my girl. Just not like that.'

The knocking persisted. This time it was a little more forceful.

Nathaniel stood up to answer it.

Milly threw her arms around him. 'No,' she commanded. 'This is our time.' She nuzzled her head into Nathaniel's neck, kissing and biting softly at him.

The Marine pushed her gently away. 'Milly. Stop it. Please.'

'Please,' she said back to him. Her voice high and loud. 'Please. Please. Please,' she taunted.

'Milly, calm down. I'm going to see who is at the door. Settle. There is no need to make a scene. You're just going to upset yourself.'

'Sure,' retorted Milly. 'Why don't you go and see who's at the door? Why don't you just go? Go again, like always.' She burst into tears.

The knocking on the door continued and someone shouted 'Hey, Nathaniel. It's me. Are you in?'

'Listen, Milly,' said Nathaniel. 'It's Roo. I'll just have a quick chat with him and then we can get back to dinner. We can talk. It'll be nice.'

'I don't want to talk anymore,' said Milly. 'Get out. Get out and never talk to me again!' she shouted.

Nathaniel threw up his hands in exasperation as he left the room. He went to the front door, opened it, and stepped outside to greet his friend.

Milly ran to the table and swept the food off it with her forearm, knocking it to the floor. Then she picked up the cherry pie and threw it against the wall.

Finally, she sat down, her breath coming in huge gasps, tears streaming down her face. She picked up the carving knife that was still on the table. Then she pulled up the hem of her dress to expose her thighs. The tops of her legs were covered in a welter of thick purple scars. Thirty or forty of them.

She sucked in another deep breath and then, with dreadful concentration, she drew the blade across the top of her inner thigh, cutting deeply into her flesh. She gritted her teeth against the pain and forced herself to continue the cut. It was necessary. It had to be done. She was a bad girl and needed to be punished. Perhaps, if she punished herself enough then Nathaniel would forgive her. Perhaps … even love her.

She set the blade against her skin and prepared to cut again.

CHAPTER 5

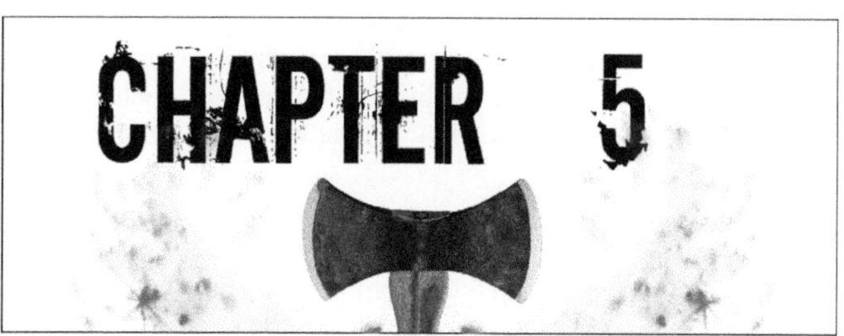

The twins both gathered firewood as the man set up a bivouac. It was proving difficult, as everything was wet. Two days had passed since that mad escape from the burning of the Orc armory. They had traveled the whole of the first night and most of the next day before resting up. This morning they had set off again, but the man had called an early stop as the weather had turned.

Heavy rain turning to sleet as the sun started to go down.

The man's name was Jack. Jack Olsen. He was in his mid-forties and before the pulse he had been a member of the British SBS or Special Boat Service, the Royal Marine version of the respected Special Air Service. During the initial stages of the Fair-Folk leadership, Jack's brother, a farmer in Devon, had been hung for dissent. He had refused to trade with the Fair-Folk, insisting that his crops would go to humans first.

From that day on, Jack had carried out a one-man program of resistance. He burned down buildings, poisoned wells, set traps for Orc patrols, and driven off their cattle and burned their crops. Sometimes he would strike two or three times in a row and then, sometimes he would simply lie low for weeks, even months at a time. After talking to him for a while, the twins came to realize that the ex-special forces man seemed less driven by revenge than the fact that he simply did not know what else to do with his life. The sabotage and retribution was no longer a means to an end, it had become the end in itself. A reason to wake up every day. To eat. To sleep. To stay alive.

Jack was no longer fighting a war. He was no longer even seeking revenge. He was simply continuing to do the only thing that he knew how to do. But, despite all of that, he did it very well.

The boys carried their collection of firewood back to the camp and piled it in front of Jack. The ex-soldier had pulled two young trees down and lashed them to a stake in the ground, creating a rain resistant area under them. It wasn't waterproof, but it did keep the bulk of the rain out. He had also strung up a tarpaulin against a large rock and that area was waterproof, as well as being protected from the wind.

He started a small fire under the tree shelter and, within a short time, had the damp wood burning merrily, albeit smokily. The twins sat close to the flames for warmth as Jack spitted three rabbits over the fire.

'So, boys,' said Jack as he turned the rabbits. 'Have you ever heard of the Scottish Free State?'

Donny chuckled. 'Yeah. Also, Eldorado and Atlantis.'

'No,' said Jack. 'I'm serious. It's real. It's the other side of Hadrian's Wall. No Orcs or goblins or Fair-Folk. No bleeding worthy humans either.'

'Come on, Jack,' argued Donny. 'It's a fairytale. A myth. There's no Free State. The Fair-Folk wouldn't let it exist.'

'It does exist,' insisted Jack. 'I met a guy who knew someone who had been there. Apparently, a king rules it and everyone gets land and a house with running water and meat and bread and clothes. It's true.'

'Well,' said Lonny. 'I heard that it's run by an immortal demigod who can do magic and he carries a huge war axe and controls thunder and lightning and he traveled through time to save the human race.'

'Actually,' said Jack. 'I must admit, I heard that as well.'

Donny sighed. 'Would be nice if it was true,' he said. Both Jack and Lonny laughed. 'Yep,' they agreed.

'That would be nice.'

'I'll tell you something that is true,' continued Jack. 'And this I know because I've actually been there. About ten years ago, but still. It's a place called the abbey. A sort of farming collective run by an ex-soldier. A guy called Axel. He doesn't allow worthy humans in the collective and he makes all Orcs and goblins and Fair-Folk stay outside the farm limits.'

'Really?' asked Lonny skeptically.

'Really,' affirmed Jack. 'I think that we should head there. It would be nice to be a part of something again. Be normal. Sleep in a bed. Belong.'

The twins nodded. 'Okay, Jack. Let's do it. Do you know the way?'

'I do.'

The next morning the three companions headed off with a purpose.

***

Seth Hil-Nu took a sip of the ice-cold sherbet, savoring the taste of orange, lime, peach, and rose petals. Like most of the Fair-Folk he had become hopelessly addicted to the fruit and flower petal-based drinks, the combination effecting his alien makeup in much the same way that alcohol effected humans.

Commander Ammon drank only fresh water. At room temperature.

'This so-called Free State worries me,' he said.

'No need,' said Seth. 'We patrol the area in front of the wall, and to my knowledge, hardly any humans even know that it exists.'

'True,' agreed Ammon. 'But I sense great power beyond the wall. And I like not the rumors of the human they call The Forever Man.'

'Stuff and nonsense,' insisted Seth. 'Myths started by a desperate people who clutch at straws.'

'Yet their mages manage to keep you out,' countered Ammon.

'True,' admitted Seth. 'They have some talent with shielding. But we shall penetrate their shields. It is merely a question of time. I have instructed the magic circle to change their tactics. Now, instead of bludgeoning away at them we have adopted a more insidious approach. We have flooded the area with subtle power and wait for it to seep in, to find the smallest of cracks in their defense and slowly ease its way through. Like water breaking a rock. Slowly but surely.'

'How long?' asked Ammon.

'Not long,' assured Seth. 'Not long.'

Ammon sighed in exasperation. 'Not long is an unacceptable time frame,' he said. 'I need a firmer commitment, senior mage. In the meantime, I am going to send a small team to attempt to achieve clandestine observation.

Perhaps even sneak in past the human sentries.'

Seth raised an eyebrow in disbelief. 'But, Commander. That would be placing one of the Fair-Folk in great danger. Do you really think that the risk versus the reward warrants such a step?'

'I will not send one of us,' replied Ammon.

'But, who else? We cannot trust any of the humans. Even the worthies are not beyond reproach. To be honest, we still aren't that sure how these people think. They are illogical, stubborn and contrary.'

'I wasn't thinking of humans either. I was thinking of sending a single Orc. I plan on sending Sergeant Kob.'

'The strange Orc?' questioned Seth. 'I have heard of him. Some say that he should have been put down. He fits not the mold, and I have heard tell, that he thinks. Actually thinks as opposed to simply obeying. The pit masters say that he is an abnormality brought on by Orcs associating too closely with humans. It has clouded the replication magiks and resulted in a faulty reproduction.'

'I agree,' said Ammon. 'But I feel that his abnormalities might be put to our advantage. I have spoken to him and he grasped the concept of a clandestine operation instantly, something that no other Orc would be capable of. Also, he claims to have met the so-called Forever Man. In fact, he engaged him in single combat.'

'Really? What did he have to say about him?'

Ammon shrugged. 'Orcs are not given to great skill with their verbal expression. He simply said that the human was a good fighter.'

'So, what made him think that he was facing the mythical Forever Man?'

He claimed that the human he fought was faster and stronger than him, as well as being able to absorb more physical punishment.'

'Never,' scoffed Seth. 'Thin skins could never out-muscle an Orc. It's impossible.'

'Exactly,' agreed Ammon. 'But Orcs have never been known to lie. So now I hope that you can appreciate my concern a little more.'

'I do, my old friend,' replied Seth. 'Indeed, I do.' The mage downed the rest of his sherbet and shuddered nervously.

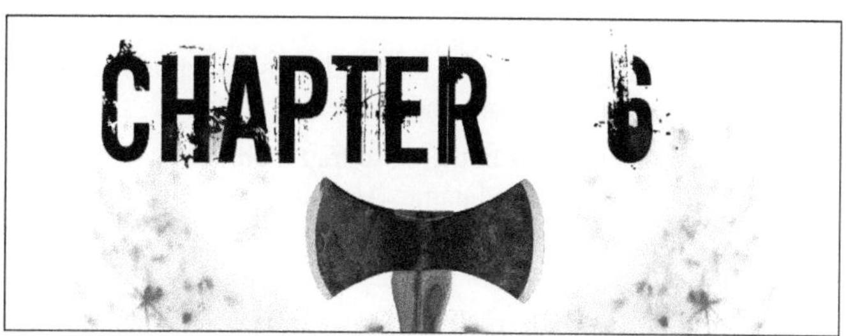

CHAPTER 6

There were sixty of them. They were equally distributed between the ten strange looking craft that they rode in. Six men in each. The craft were constructed of wooden planks bound together in the overlapping caravel method and were fashioned with a low, wide profile and had two long outriggers, one per side. A single lugsail stood high on each vessel.

The rig was perfectly suited to skimming across the ice and slush that the Irish Sea had become since the global cooling that had followed the pulse. It also sailed well across any open water that it came to.

This was no fishing smack. There were no nets and no derricks for lifting. But there was a fair-sized hold. Because this was a craft designed with only one purpose in mind—raiding.

Getting in fast, loading up with spoils and getting out.

***

Angus Hume set his last game snare on the top of the cliffs overlooking Portavaddie, stood up, stretched, and stared out at the Irish Sea. As usual, visibility was down to less than a mile, confounded by the perpetual fog that lurked above the icy surface. Small fishing boats could venture a mile or so out to sea before they came up against solid sheets of ice and the broken teeth of countless small icebergs.

Still, even in those conditions, the fishing was spectacularly good with fish stocks having increased tenfold since the pulse had put a cessation to all industrial scale commercial fishing. As a result, the village was relatively well off, in the scheme of things. Food was plentiful; they had a brisk trade in smoked fish, bonemeal, and fish oil, and wanted for nothing.

The main reason that Angus bothered to trap rabbits was to offer the villagers a choice between fish and game. Also, he cured the fur and sold the pelts to widow MacGeekie who made mittens that were in big demand in the interior.

In fact, it would be safe to say that Portavaddie was one of the few places that was doing much better after the pulse than before.

And then, in the distance, Angus saw what looked like a group of water striders. Low and flat with two long legs sticking out either side. As they got closer he recognized them for what they were. Some sort of sail-powered craft.

They moved with a particular grace and speed, skimming across the ice and water like they were hovering above it, and in no time at all, they had pulled up onto the beach below the village.

The men disembarked swiftly and formed up on the beach. Four men in front and behind them, eight rows of seven. Even at the distance that Angus was he could see that the men were well armed. Short swords and long spears, perhaps eight foot in length. But the most striking part of their weaponry were their shields. Round in shape and covered in highly polished gold, each one reflecting back the pulse light in an orgasm of color.

They started to march towards the village and Angus' heart sank. It was patently obvious from the marching men's demeanor that this was no trade delegation. There would be neither offer of payment nor talk of deals. These were men who had come to take what they wanted by blade and by fist.

These were raiders.

Angus dropped his snares and water flask, drew his short sword, and ran as fast as he could down the rugged mountain track, slipping and sliding as he did, his old limbs unequal to the task but his fear and anger driving him hard nonetheless.

***

Effemy Gordania sat on a bale of straw. In front of her sat her students. Mister bunny, Patrick the postman, wooden dog and Raggie rag doll. She had fashioned chairs out of lengths of kindling and the stable wall behind her served as her blackboard.

Today she was teaching her toys mathematics and wooden dog was being particularly obtuse. But Effemy was a good teacher, kind and patient. Much like her mother, who in actuality, was the real village teacher and was tasked with teaching the children of Portavaddie their three R's.

But today was a Sunday so there was no school. In fact, there wasn't much of anything, Sunday being well observed in Portavaddie, a village that had more churches than it did pubs.

But before Effemy could explain the math problem to wooden dog in more detail, she was interrupted by the sounds of shouting. Grown up shouting. Men's voices. Guttural and incoherent. Shouting for shouting's sake. Not for communication.

Then she heard another sound. It was a sound that she had never heard before, so she got up from her hay bale and walked around the corner to take a look.

The sound that she had never heard before was the sound of metal striking metal. Of blade clashing against blade as the surprised men of Portavaddie fought for their lives. And the lives of their families.

And then the shouting turned to screams of agony and yells of terror as the raiders started to decimate the civilian population. There seemed to be no answer to their long spears. And they moved as one. Close drilled and deadly, golden shield to golden shield, spears stabbing, swords hacking, and boots trampling.

The main street ran red with the free-flowing of blood and gore and the raiders split up to seek out more victims. A group of seven raiders ran past Effemy, ignoring her completely.

The little girl ran back to her classroom and gathered up her toys. 'Quiet,' she urged them. 'Don't worry. I'll keep you safe. We'll hide in the stables.'

Effemy ran into the stables, went to the back, and burrowed into the piles of hay, covering herself completely.

She held wooden dog's mouth shut as they all lay still, because she knew that wooden dog was very scared and wanted to cry. But she also knew that he mustn't or else the bad men would find them and stab them with their long spears and make their blood spill out of them.

'Quiet,' she whispered to wooden dog. 'Be very quiet.'

***

Angus lay with his back against the wall, legs splayed out in front of him like a child at play. His short sword lay broken and notched at his side. He had been stabbed in the shoulder and his left leg. The bleeding had eased but he simply did not seem to have enough energy to move himself, try as he might. And, to be honest, he didn't really care anymore. He was old, he had put up a good fight and there was no shame in simply slipping away.

He heard a slight sound and looked up to see a little girl standing in front of him. She was holding a carved wooden dog with felt ears.

'Hello, sweety,' he croaked.

'Hello,' she replied. 'Are you sore?'

Angus nodded. 'A little bit,' he admitted.

'Everyone is dead,' answered Effemy.

Angus peered around him. It appeared that the little girl was correct. Strangely the raiders had not set fire to everything. They had systematically gone through every house and removed anything of value that they could find. Cutlery, coins, weapons, fine clothing, and blankets. Preserved food.

They had left the village a lifeless worthless hulk.

When he turned his head back the little girl was gone. But within minutes she returned, carrying a sewing basket. She opened it and pulled out various lengths of bandage.

'Here,' she said. 'Let's try to make you better.'

Angus took a deep breath, and for the little girl's sake, he made himself care again.

'You're Catriona's girl, aren't you?' asked Angus. 'What's your name?'

'Effemy.'

'Pretty name,' said Angus. 'It means "Good Speaker." Did you know that?'

Effemy nodded. 'Daddy says that I'm always speaking. He says that he should have named me Shysie 'cause it means "Silence," then maybe I wouldn't talk so much.'

Angus chuckled. 'Maybe. Effemy, could you help me here? Hold your finger on the bandage while I tie it tight.'

The old man pulled the bandage tight on his leg, and then after a few attempts at strapping his shoulder wound he gave up. The angle was too awkward, and although Effemy tried to help she wasn't strong enough to bind the bandage tightly enough. Eventually, Angus simply fashioned a sling from the length of linen, so that at least, he could take the weight off his arm and keep it semi-immobilized.

'Can we go and find my mommy and daddy now?' asked Effemy.

'Where is your house?' enquired Angus.

The little girl pointed down the road. 'Last one on the left. With the green door.'

Angus pulled himself to his feet, wincing at the pain as he did so. 'I tell you what, Effemy my sweet,' he said. 'You wait here with your dog and I'll go and take a quick look for your parents. Okay?'

Effemy nodded and the old man limped down the street towards the house. He glanced at the bodies sprawled alongside the road as he walked, checking to see if any might be alive. But the long spears had dealt wounds of such savagery and depth as to have ensured death. He marveled that he was still alive and put it down to the fact that his wounds probably looked more life-threatening than they actually were.

The green door to Effemy's house was open and he stepped inside, waiting on the threshold for a few seconds to allow his eyes to adjust to the interiors gloom.

Effemy's father lay on his back in the middle of the sitting room. He had died badly, his torso and face a mass of deep cuts. In his right hand he held a bloodied knife, so he must have stabbed someone at least.

The little girl's mother lay at the bottom of the stairs.

Her throat had been cut.

Her dress was still ruched up around her waist and her legs were sprawled open exposing her nakedness to the uncaring world.

Angus pulled her dress down to cover her. Then he closed her eyes.

He shut the door behind him as he left the house and limped back to Effemy.

He knelt down in front of her and gathered her into his arms, ignoring the pain of his shoulder wound.

'I'm sorry, sweety,' he said. 'Mommy and daddy have gone to heaven.'

Effemy said nothing but the old man could feel her tears running down his cheek and onto his neck.

Angus held her until she stopped crying then he stood up and took her hand.

'Come on then, little one,' he said. 'We need to get to the village of Glenan Burn to get help and to spread the news about this.'

And the two of them set off towards the cliffs, leaving the dead village behind them.

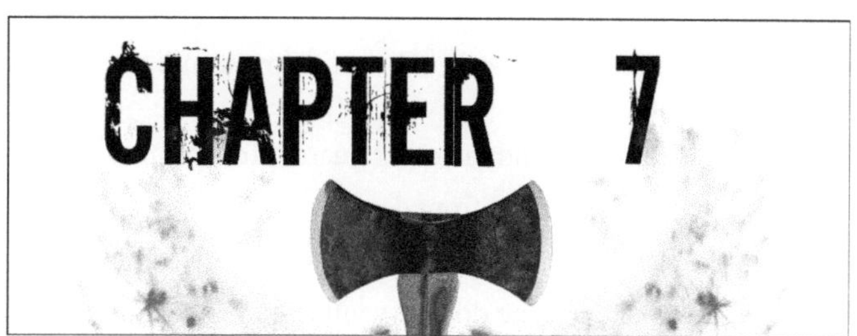

The three travelers stopped at the gate and the twins stood still while Jack walked forward to present himself to the guards.

There was a brief conversation and then Jack beckoned to the twins.

'Come on, boys,' he said. 'We're in.'

The boys trudged after the ex-SBS soldier and one of the guards who had led them through the gate. It had been a tough three weeks since the burning of the Orc armory. They had stayed out of sight and lived off the land. Jack had indulged in two more small acts of sabotage along the way. He had thrown a dead sheep's carcass into a well and he had laid a series of spiked traps along a trail that the Orcs often used. Traps that simply consisted of a hole about a foot deep, wide enough for an Orc's foot to fit into, with a sharpened wooden spike set into the bottom. The hole would then be covered over with grass or twigs to conceal.

But, in the main, they had simply slogged northwards looking for the abbey.

And, that evening, they had finally found it and had sneaked past the Orc encampment on its borders.

After a few minutes of walking they came to another gate. This one was set into a high stone wall. It looked ancient but well kept. The gate was open and flanked by yet more armed guards.

Their guard beckoned for them to continue following and they did so without talking.

He headed for the main building, a large stone edifice, five stories high. When he got to the front door he handed them over to the two guards standing there.

'Newcomers,' he told the guards. 'One of them ex-military so I brought them to see the captain.'

The new guards nodded, and the other guard left to return to his post.

One of the guards opened the front door.

'Come on,' he said as he walked in. The three followed him.

The door opened into a large double-vaulted entrance hall. A fire crackled in a huge hearth. Carpets covered the wooden floor and candles in wall sconces lit the room.

'Wait here,' ordered the guard as he left, walking down the long adjoining corridor and entering a room at the very end.

The three travelers stood close to the fire, holding their hands out for warmth. They stood silently. Waiting. Jack seemed to be at ease, but the young twin brothers were obviously nervous. Wary of what might happen next.

After a while the door at the end of the corridor opened and the guard called out to them.

'Come on down. The captain will see you now.'

He showed the trio in and then left, closing the door as he did so.

Jack and the twins found themselves in a large study. Wood paneling, fireplace, scattered Chesterfield chairs, and a desk with a man sitting behind it.

The man stood to greet them and walked around the desk, hand outstretched.

He was around six foot tall, a neatly trimmed beard and moustache, brown with streaks of gray. He wore an eye patch over his right eye and a massive scar crawled down his face from temple to lip. His neck was thick with muscle and he moved with the surefootedness and confidence of a warrior.

He shook Jack's hand first and then moved on to Lonny and Donny.

'Greetings, travelers,' he said. 'My name is Axel. I am the commanding officer of the abbey. You may call me Axel, or Captain or Chief if you prefer.'

'Corporal Jack Olsen, sir,' responded Jack. 'SBS. X squadron.'

Axel smiled. 'By strength and guile, hey Corporal,' he said, quoting the SBS motto.

'That's us, sir. These two youngsters are Lonny and Donny. Twins. Teamed up with them after we met back in Devon.'

The twins mumbled their greetings.

'So then,' continued Axel. 'What have you all been up to of late and what brings you here, to the abbey?'

'Simply looking for a place to belong, sir,' answered Jack. 'Become a little tired of wandering, living off the land.'

'And you two,' enquired Axel of the twins. 'You look a little young to have grown tired of anything. And where are your parents, your family?'

'Parents are dead, sir,' answered Donny. 'No brothers or sisters. No other relatives as far as I know. Just us.'

'And how did you all meet?'

The twins stood silently, a slightly panicked look on their faces. Jack simply stood at ease, his features blank. Expressionless.

'Come on, then,' continued Axel. 'Out with it. We're all friends here, and friends don't keep secrets.'

Jack spoke first. 'We were burning down an Orc armory, sir.'

Axel raised an eyebrow. 'What, all of you?'

'Well not initially,' continued Jack. 'I went into the garrison with intent to burn the armory down and I met these two already inside the wall. They were carrying a sack full of rotten rats. They were going to chuck them down the well. Poisoning the water.'

Axel laughed. 'Not a bad plan. Might have worked.' Jack nodded. 'Might have, if they didn't get caught.

Anyhow, I convinced them to join me and we torched the place and ran. Been together ever since.'

'Well met then, I say,' said Axel. 'Gentlemen, there is definitely a place for you all here at the abbey. We shall supply digs, probably shared, and there is plenty of work. There are no idle hands in the abbey, we work hard and look out for each other. I'll have the guard show you to the guest rooms. I have a couple of old friends staying there at the moment but there is room enough for all, and I am sure that you'll get on. It's an old lady, name of Gramma Higgins, show her a shedload of respect and she may not beat you to death. Also, her granddaughter, Janeka. Nice girl.'

Axel walked to the door and bellowed for the guard who came running.

'Jakobs,' he said. 'Take these gentlemen to the guest rooms. Introduce them to Gramma and make sure they are fed and watered.'

The guard ripped off a crisp salute and motioned for the trio to follow him.

Axel closed his door without a farewell.

***

Jack pushed his plate away, leant back in his chair and belched softly. The twins sniggered.

'Sorry,' apologized the ex-soldier. 'It's just that I haven't eaten that well in years. Literally.'

Gramma Higgins laughed. 'Dat be fine, child,' she said. 'Always better out dan in, I always say. Better out dan in. Janeka,' she shouted for her granddaughter. 'Bring da brandy and some glasses for da boys.'

Janeka came in from the kitchen carrying a bottle and four mugs. She set them down on the table and poured a generous measure of spirits into each one, passing one to her grandmother, one to Jack, and the other two for the twins.

'So, you boys planning on settling down here?'

Jack nodded. 'Seems like a nice enough place. Our second choice really. We actually wanted to find the Free State.'

'Yeah,' laughed Donny. 'You know, the one that's ruled over by an immortal king who wields and axe and can make lightning.'

The three men laughed.

'Oh, you be talking about Nathaniel,' said Gramma. 'American. He be called The Forever Man by some. Nice man, but you don't want to get on his bad side. Saw him once, he brung down a lightning storm so fierce it almost burned an entire forest to da ground. Ain't dat so, Janeka?'

The granddaughter nodded. 'That's right, Gramma. But he was in a trance or something at the time; I believe that part of him traveled back in time to the Druidic days or something. Can't rightly remember, truth be told. It was over twenty years ago.'

'We seed him again, couple of years ago. He'd been away for twenty years, back in time. Fighting the Romans I do believe, but he didn't look a day older.'

Janeka nodded in agreement. 'Not one day. A few more scars and a long beard but not a second older.'

Gramma took a sip of her brandy. 'He was King Arthur, you know? He sure does get around dat boy. He sure does.'

The three friends stared at Gramma and her niece, their mouths open, faces pictures of almost comical amazement.

Then Jack started to laugh. 'Good one, Gramma,' he said. 'Had us going there. Very funny.'

Gramma shook her head and gave the ex-soldier a stern look. 'Don't you go calling me and my kin liars, you hear, boy,' she admonished. 'We be telling da truth, da whole truth, an' nutting but da truth, so help me.'

'Really?'

'Really,' insisted Gramma.

'So then,' continued Jack. 'Where is this Forever Man and his Free State?'

'It be da other side of the wall. Hadrian's Wall. If you can get through the Orc patrols without being caught, then those folks will welcome you wid open arms. Or so I'm told. Me, I is content wid my life. De Fair-Folks and de worthies leave me well enough alone and I pretty much ignores dem. I's too old to change and go gallivanting off to new worlds and whatever. But you boys is young. Mayhap you give it a try.'

Jack nodded. 'Mayhap we will, Gramma. Mayhap we will.'

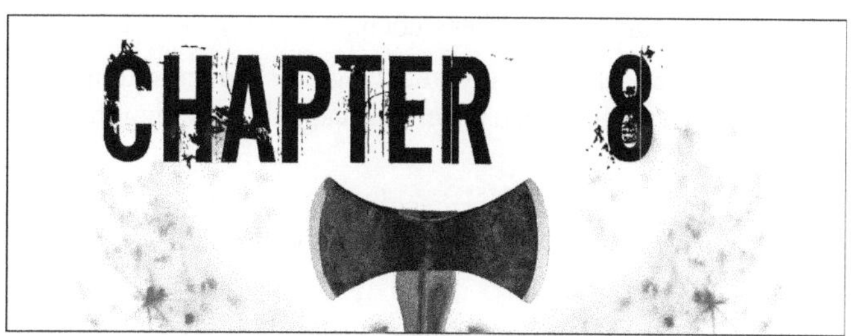

CHAPTER 8

The class of children stood up as Nathaniel entered the room. The class consisted of children of mixed ages from seven to seventeen, both male and female. But they all had two things in common. Firstly, they were all born after the pulse, and secondly, Gogo had deemed that they all had "talent." How she decided this was beyond Nathaniel, but he trusted her judgment implicitly. After all, she had been the accepted wisdom of the walking folk led by Papa Dante for more years than anyone could remember, and if her wisdom was good enough for Papa, then it was good enough for the Marine.

'Greetings, Free people,' greeted Nathaniel.

'Good morning, King Nathaniel,' they greeted back.

The Marine raised his right fist in the air. 'Oorah!' he shouted.

The children did the same, raising their clenched fists and yelling out the Marine war cry at the top of their lungs.

'OORAH!'

Nathaniel grinned, gave them a thumbs-up and followed Gogo from the room, leaving them to practice their concentration exercises while she and Nathaniel talked.

'How goes it, Gogo?' he asked.

'Slowly,' said the old blind lady. 'They all have the talent, some stronger than others, but it has been many years since I have taught anyone. And even then, it was different. There is no doubt that every one of these children are naturally stronger than me when it comes to the magik. But getting it out of them is a bit of trial and error and I have to be careful, one doesn't want too many errors. Who knows what could happen if someone inadvertently threw a fireball or bolt of lightning at another student.'

Nathaniel laughed. 'That is very true, Gogo. I shudder to think what I might have got up to if I had been a teenager capable of setting the classroom on fire with thought.'

'It's no laughing matter, Marine,' scolded Gogo. 'With all that testosterone and female hormones running riot I have to keep a very careful eye on them.'

Nathaniel nodded his understanding.

'I saw Rosie O' Donell yesterday. Do you remember me talking about her?'

Nathaniel wrinkled his brow in thought. 'Is she the young girl with two children already?'

'Aye, that's the one. A son and a daughter. Four years and three years, both second generation post-pulse. Her husband was also born post-pulse. Anyway, the kiddies already show great talent. I can feel it in them. It's uncanny. I think that, as more second generation post-pulsers come into the world we are going to see huge changes. Already the wheel is turning, time is being reeled back in and we find ourselves being drawn into an older age.'

'I am not sure what you mean, Gogo,' admitted Nathaniel.

'Magik, my king,' said Gogo. 'Look around you, what do you see?'

Nathaniel looked. 'People. Soldiers in armor, houses, horses.'

'Like we have gone back in time to the Middle Ages.'

'Yes,' admitted Nathaniel. 'But that is because of the pulse. It has nothing to do with magik.'

'You think not?' insisted Gogo. 'Pray then, Marine, tell me one thing— why are you called king?'

Nathaniel shrugged and then remembered that Gogo could not see. 'Who else would be king? I asked not for the role, the role chose me. Perhaps no one else could do it.'

'I would not argue against that, Marine,' said Gogo. 'You are the only one who could fill the role; it was something that you were destined to do from the moment that you were born. But you did not answer my question. I asked why are you called king. Why not prime minister or president or even general or chief? Why king?'

'I know not, Gogo. It simply seemed the correct form of address to adopt. People simply called me, king.'

'Aye,' agreed the old lady. 'And the way you talk now. The way everybody talks. Haven't you noticed the subtle differences to the past?'

'Again, Gogo, I am not completely sure about what you refer to.'

'Formality,' said Gogo. 'Sentence structure is changing. When people see each other they no longer say, "Yo" and high five each other. They say, "Greetings, sir" and "I bid you farewell, my lady". As I said, the wheel is turning, and time is returning to an older period. Technology will not work again for many hundreds, perhaps thousands of years. Magik will grow until it reigns supreme. We will return to the days of Merlin, of druids and sorcerers, of mages and wizards. Mark my words, king; the future is the past that is the future. Remember that well when you and your advisers plan humanities way forward. This is merely the very beginning of what will be a very long trip for you, Forever Man.'

Before Nathaniel could say anything, he was interrupted by Tad, who ran up to the two of them in obvious consternation.

'Greetings, Gogo,' he said. 'My king,' he continued. 'Sorry to barge in like this, but there is someone here that you need to see. He has just arrived this morning, on horseback and accompanied by two others. I have them waiting at your residence, boss.'

Nathaniel bowed floridly to Gogo. 'With your leave, my lady,' he said with a grin. 'I need to see to this. But I will think on what you said.'

'Gogo waved him away. 'Go. And don't forget to practice your control exercises. You too have much to learn about the talent.'

Nathaniel followed the fast-walking Tad. 'What gives, little big man?' he asked.

'It's a bit of an unbelievable story. You need to hear it yourself. This old guy came galloping in here with two younger escorts. The old guy has been quite severely wounded, but he said that he had to see you to report in person. Said that he owed it to Effemy, whoever that might be.'

When they got to Nathaniel's residence the three men were waiting in the entrance hall. Chairs had been provided but they had elected to stand. They drew themselves to attention as the Marine entered the hallway.

'Please, good people,' said Nathaniel. 'Be at ease. Come, follow me to my study. Tad, organize some refreshments, water, fruit juice, some bread and cheese. Also, some brandy. Many thanks.'

Tad hurried off to do Nathaniel's bidding and the three men followed the Marine down the hallway to his study. Nathaniel sat in a wingback chair and gestured for the others to sit on the sofas opposite him.

'Right, gentlemen,' he said. 'Talk to me.'

'My king,' began the older wounded man. 'My name is Angus Hume. I live in the fishing village of Portavaddie.'

'I have heard of it,' said Nathaniel. 'Much of our fish oil for the lamps comes from there.'

A flicker of pride sparked in Angus' eyes and he nodded. 'Aye, it would. We do …did … good quality fish oil.'

'You say, did,' enquired the Marine.

'Yes, my king. The truth of the matter is—Portavaddie is no more. Three days ago, we were attacked by raiders. They came from across the Irish Sea in craft that skimmed across both ice and water. Armed with spears and sword were they. Well drilled and merciless. We fought as hard as we could, my lord, but only I and little Effemy lived. They slaughtered everybody else. They killed, they raped, and they plundered all that we had of value and then they left. I only survived because they took me for dead. Effemy hid under the hay and they missed her. I came to tell my king, as quickly as I could. The neighboring villages have started a town watch, sire. But we are mere fishermen. These raiders were trained warriors and I fear, that if … nay, when they strike again, the result will be just as horrific.' The old man went down on one knee. 'Help us, my king. I beg of you.'

Nathaniel got to his feet. 'Stand, brave Angus of Portavaddie. You have shown great courage and fortitude. And I tell you this, there is no need to beg protection from me. I shall ride within the day with a full battle group and I swear to you, Angus Hume of Portavaddie, the Free People will be protected, and we shall exact retribution on these so-called raiders.'

Angus grasped Nathaniel's hand and kissed it, tears rolling down his wrinkled cheeks. 'Thank you, lord. Thank you.'

'Now rest, all of you,' continued Nathaniel. 'Tad will be back shortly with sustenance. I want you all to eat your fill and then rest. You will achieve nothing if you all pass out from exhaustion. Worry not. I shall wake you before we leave.'

Angus stayed kneeling on the floor and the two younger men bowed deeply as Nathaniel left the room, closing the door behind him.

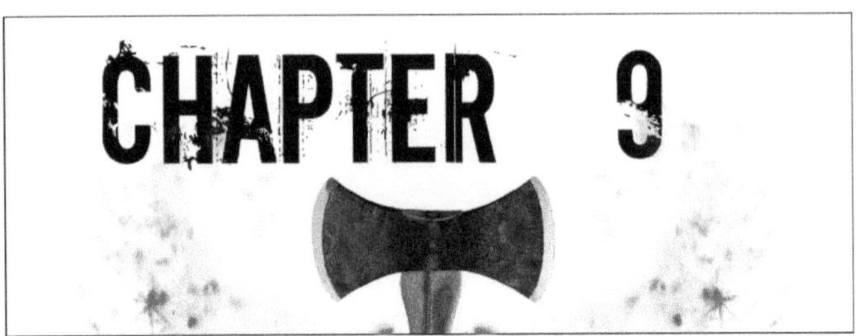

CHAPTER 9

Axel leant back in his chair and smiled. 'Yes,' he confirmed. 'All of those stories that Gramma and Janeka told you are true. And there are more. I saw him almost single-handedly take out over fifty well-armed, highly dangerous enemies. Okay, he did have a machine gun and a pistol, but the last dozen or so he dispatched with an axe. It was like watching a hurricane destroy an island. Elemental.' Axel shook his head. 'Never seen anything like it before or since.'

'We would all very much like to go to the Free State, sir,' said Jack.

Axel nodded. 'And I have no doubt that you would do very well there. Life is hard but fair and simple. However, there is every chance that, in the foreseeable future, the Fair-Folk will declare out and out war with the Free State. If so, King Nathaniel will find himself attempting to repel over two million Orcs and goblins as well as the power of the Fair-Folk mages. You may very well find that you have jumped from the frying pan into the proverbial fire. What then?'

'We would fight,' said Jack, and the twins added their approval. 'Anyway, Gramma told us that he had already fought the Fair-Folk once and won against overwhelming odds.'

'That is true,' admitted Axel. 'But he took them by surprise. And they did not press the attack. Imagine fighting that same battle … then imagine extending it out for another month. Two months. A year. Do you still think that he might win?'

Jack shrugged. 'With all due respect, sir, a soldier does not fight merely because he thinks that he will definitely win. Winning is not the be all and end all, sir.

'We would fight even if we knew that we would lose. We would fight because we are human. They are not. And who knows what might happen. We might win.'

'And if it were anyone else that we were talking about I would laugh in your face, Corporal,' said Axel. 'But, when it comes to The Forever Man, all things are possible.'

'So, sir,' continued Jack. 'Will you help the boys and me to get there?'

'I will, soldier, I will. But before you set off please let me put forward a proposal. And in no way must you feel under any pressure, I am proposing, not commanding.'

Jack nodded. 'Go ahead, sir.'

'Why wait? Why not start to fight right now. Right here?'

'I'm sorry, sir,' responded Jack. 'I'm not sure that I understand.'

'I am sure that you agree with me when I say that, ultimately, war against the Fair-Folk is inevitable. Normally I wouldn't speak so freely but, knowing your background I feel that I can.'

Jack nodded. 'The country is big enough for all of us but I'm not sure the Free-Folk see it that way, so, yes, ultimately war is inevitable,' agreed Jack.

'So why should we wait for them to strike?' asked Axel.

'Because to strike now would be premature, sir. They would obliterate us. It makes no military sense whatsoever.'

'I agree, Corporal. But I'm not talking about open warfare. What I'm talking about is merely an increase in what you have already been doing. Sabotage, subterfuge. Wrecking communications, firing armories, poisoning grain stores, setting booby traps. A constant low-level campaign to make the country ungovernable.'

Jack sat in silence for a while as did the twins. Eventually he spoke. 'There would be reprisals,' he said.

'Against who,' retaliated Axel.

'Anyone,' said Jack. 'Everyone. The pig-faces would go mental. Public hangings, floggings.'

'Is that a bad thing?' questioned the captain.

'It is if you're the poor bugger being hung,' answered Jack.

'I know this sounds harsh,' said Axel. 'But, in the long run, it would stiffen human resolve. It would turn the fence-sitters and invigorate the masses. Sometimes sacrifices need to be made. Jack, I want to put you in charge of a new branch of my army. A new SBS if you would. Young, keen men who will put themselves on the line for the sake of humanity and its future. Will you do it?'

'Is this The Forever Man's idea, sir,' enquired Jack.

Axel shook his head. 'It's not really the way that he thinks. If I proposed this to him he would insist on trying to do it all himself. And then he would run around the country personally attempting to save everyone who got involved with the scheme. Like a tornado ripping through a wheat field, he would leave a path of destruction behind him that would far exceed the damage that he was trying to prevent in the first place. Like I said before—he is an elemental force, there is little subtlety about him.'

'Whatever?' said Lonny. 'I'm in.'

'Me too,' affirmed Donny.

Jack turned to face them. 'No, you are not,' he snapped. 'This isn't a game, boys. You've been involved in one minor skirmish and you think that you're the bee's knees. Whoever gets involved in this resistance movement is in for a rough ride. Many will die, and they will die badly. Torture, degradation, and death. It will not be pretty.' He turned to face Axel. 'I'll do it. But with one stipulation—the boys get taken to the Free State. I won't have their blood on my hands.'

Lonny jumped to his feet. 'All due respect, Jack,' he shouted. 'You do not have the authority to make bargains with us. Donny and I will do it. And we will do it with or without you. You are not our father. And do you know why? Because our father is dead. So is our mother. Dead because of the Fair-Folk and their pig-faced soldiers. Do not deny us retribution, Jack. Please. Don't do that.'

Jack stared at the boy for a while. Then he looked at Donny. 'You agree with him?'

Donny nodded. 'Of course.'

The ex SBS operative took a deep breath. 'Okay, Captain,' he said. 'God help me but we're all in. So how do we start?'

'First, I'd like you to meet some of the men that I have short-listed for your platoon,' said Axel. 'The final choices will be left up to you. Come on,' the captain walked towards the door. 'Let's go.'

CHAPTER 10

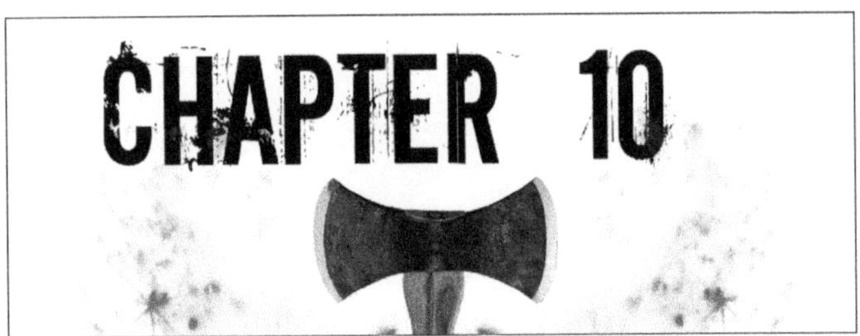

The unicorn stood at the top of the mountain of Ben Hope and surveyed the land around it. Behind lay Loch Hope. To its left, Loch na Seilg. To the front, looking west, the Strathmore River and the great Loch Meadie.

It sniffed the air, testing for any odor of the great enemy and then, finding none, it set its sense to revealing the ley lines. The silver threads of magical power that crossed the countryside, linking all places of magical potential. It was through these lines that the unicorn could travel. It was also via these lines of power that The Forever Man would eventually come to see his full potential. To realize his true name and rise to wield the power that the universe had gifted him.

But that would not be for a while. And, perhaps, mused the unicorn, it may never come to pass. Because the future was a constantly changing thing. Ephemeral and entropic, meaning that it was impossible to predict with any type of accuracy, because the mere act of divination changed one's perception and thereby changed the predicted future. But it was possible to guide. To shepherd the future in a general direction. This was, and always had been, the unicorn's purpose. Its sole purpose. And, although it knew not the intimate details of the coming future, it did know one thing for certain …

It knew that, without The Forever Man, there were no futures at all.

Not a one.

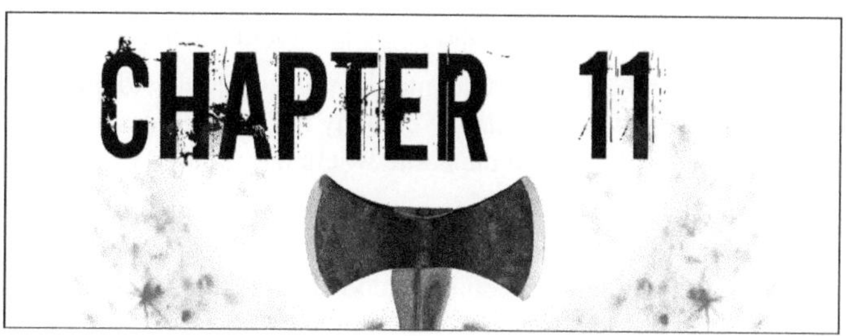

True to his word The Forever Man had left for Portavaddie that afternoon. He left with Tad and the rest of The Ten, an elite group of warriors who doubled as Nathaniel's personal guard. Like him, they all wore full armor and carried either broadsword or axe and a bundle of throwing javelins. But unlike the Marine's pitch-black armor theirs was deep, blood red.

But they would not be the only warriors going to the Portavaddie area. Readying themselves for travel for the next morning were another two thousand of the elite cavalry. Nathaniel had taken the threat very seriously and he aimed to keep the people of the Free State safe, no matter what the cost.

He and The Ten set off at a fast trot and, when the sun dropped below the horizon, they stopped for a quick cold meal and then Nathaniel conjured up a vast ball of white fire. The ball danced in front of them when they rode, lighting the landscape in eerie blue-white light. Like a hundred moons.

'Good trick,' said Tad.

'Thanks. You should see my juggling skills,' quipped the Marine.

They rode through the night, arriving at Glenan Burn, the closest village to the decimated Portavaddie, an hour after sunrise.

Because it was a fishing village, most everybody was already up. Food was being sold alongside the main street and grocers, cobblers, and butchers were setting up stalls in the square preparing for market day.

However, there was also a group of around thirty men, armed with a variety of weapons ranging from spears and swords, to wood-axes and pitchforks. This was obviously the newly formed village militia, put together in case of a visit from the raiders. One look at them was enough to tell

Nathaniel that they would be keen and brave and totally ineffectual.

When the king and The Ten rode into the village people stopped what they were doing and cheered loudly. Eventually the town alderman presented himself and showed Nathaniel to his home where they could talk.

'We have another two thousand cavalry arriving within a day,' Nathaniel told the alderman. 'I haven't worked out how we shall deploy them, but by the time they arrive I will have. Tell me, good alderman, is this the first time that this sort of raid has happened?'

'As far as I know, my king,' affirmed the alderman. 'But there have been rumors of the golden shields being seen before, sailing along the coast but never actually landing.'

'The golden shields?' enquired Tad.

'Yes, sir,' said the alderman. 'They carry round gold shields, hence the name.'

'If they attack again,' said Nathaniel. 'Where do you think that might be?'

'Oh, I would say Port Stanraer. It's one of the few places richer than Portavaddie was and it's not far from here.'

Nathaniel pulled out a map and laid it on the table. It took him a few moments to orientate himself and then he put his finger on Port Stanraer.

'Looks possible. What about here?'

The alderman nodded. 'They could strike here, lord. Also, Campbelltown, Portpatrick, and Skelmorlie. There aren't many other towns of note along this stretch of coast. Even before the pulse we were sparsely populated and since … well, there's a lot of open space.'

The Forever Man thought for a while then he came to a decision.

'Come on,' he said to Tad. 'We need to get to the top of the cliffs. I'm going to try something.'

He went outside, mounted up and rode out of the village towards the high cliff tops to the south. Tad and the rest of The Ten followed. It took twenty minutes to ride to the top of the cliffs and when they arrived, Nathaniel dismounted and walked to the very edge, peering out at the ocean and its ever-present misty cover.

'Why's it always misty?' he asked Tad.

The little big man shrugged. 'Not sure. Roo says that it has something to do with the warm air coming off the land and hitting the ice. Makes fog.'

'The air isn't that warm,' argued Nathaniel. 'Especially during winter.'

'It's warmer than ice,' countered Tad. 'True.'

Everyone stood in silence for a while. Their king was there for a reason and no one wanted to distract him. Eventually, The Forever Man went down on one knee and held his right arm out towards the open sea, his palm facing upwards, fingers stretched out, his eyes closed. He breathed slowly, and Tad could see that he was deep in concentration.

The Marine stayed down on one knee, not moving a muscle for over half an hour. Then, abruptly, he stood up.

'They're coming,' he said as he strode towards his horse. 'The alderman was correct. They're heading for Port Stanraer.'

'How many?' asked Tad.

'Not sure. Lots, maybe one hundred people. Maybe more. It's the first time that I've tried this whole far-sensing thing. I don't actually see what is happening, it's more like a strong feeling. I can feel multiple minds, some in charge, others not. But most are thinking of Port Stanraer, so I guess that's where they are heading.'

Everyone mounted and followed Nathaniel at a gallop as they thundered up the coastal track towards Port Stanraer and the raiders.

'We'll be outnumbered ten to one,' said Tad. 'You think?' answered the Marine sarcastically.

'Only making a point,' responded Tad. 'No need to get all snippy at me.'

They galloped past the outskirts of the town and down towards the main beach and harbor. Groups of amazed township dwellers came running out of residences and workplaces to gawk at the warriors as they thundered past. They pulled up at the beach and the Marine ran a soldier's eye over the terrain. Being a Marine also gave him insight into the minds of the men who would be sailing the strange craft and he immediately picked out their best landing area.

'There,' he pointed at a spot on the beach where it shelved gently upwards. It was also protected by a small spit and was close to the town. 'That is where they will land.' He continued to study the layout. 'We will place our ranks there. On that small hill.'

'Ranks,' snorted Tad. 'I wouldn't actually consider ten soldiers as ranks of men.'

Nathaniel wheeled his horse to face Tad and the rest of The Ten.

'Men,' he shouted. 'Today we will once again be tested. We face a band of raiders from across the sea.

'There are many of them. At least one hundred, perhaps more. But we are The Ten, so we shall outnumber them one to ten. We are all privileged men— for today we get to protect the innocent with our blood. We get to sacrifice ourselves to protect those who cannot protect themselves. Today will be a day for heroes. OORAH!'

As one, The Ten cheered back. 'OORAH!'

They galloped together towards the low hill that Nathaniel had pointed out, and as they got there, the raiders' skimmers appeared, like coalescing wraiths emerging from the mist. The boats ground onto the shore where Nathaniel had predicted. But there were many more than he had foreseen. As before, each craft held six men, but instead of twenty crafts as the Marine had anticipated there were at least thirty. One hundred and eighty men all told.

'Well,' said Tad, sotto voce. 'I suppose that now we outnumber them by one to eighteen. Hoo-bloody-rah.'

The Marine gave him a wink. 'No worries, my friend.

You scared or something?'

'Absolutely crapping myself,' admitted the little big man.

The Marine laughed out loud. 'Wait for them, men' he commanded. 'As soon as they form up, ready your javelins and follow me.'

The Ten loosened their javelins in their quivers and waited for the king's command.

Nathaniel judged the moment finely. The raiders had not noticed the small group of riders on the hill and they were taking their time to form up into solid ranks, their remarkable golden shields flashing in the sunlight.

'Pretty,' mumbled Tad to himself.

When the Marine considered them to be at their most unorganized he drew a javelin from his quiver, held it above his head and charged, screaming out the Marine battle cry as he did.

'Oorah!'

The ten swept down on the raiders, rapidly coming within throwing distance of them. As one they unleashed their javelins, and in a movement brought from many hours of practice, turned smoothly away. Then they formed up and charged again, unleashing their payload, and wheeling away in the same manner.

The raiders careful ranking collapsed into chaos. They had not expected any resistance at this point and already at least five lay dead and as many injured.

The Ten wheeled and threw again, and again, and again, until they had each released all ten of their javelins. Over one hundred steel tipped messengers of death had struck the ranks of the raiders. At least forty of them were either dead, dying, or totally incapacitated, and already the beach sand was stained a dark pink from the vast amounts of spilled blood.

But the raiders were well drilled, and they rallied quickly, reforming into ranks, building a shield wall and presenting their long spears outwards.

The Ten milled about the beach as their horses bucked and whinnied, not keen to charge at a wall of sharpened steel.

'Dismount,' shouted Nathaniel. 'We'll take them on foot. Tad, with me, front and center. Arrow formation, people. Someone tries to poke you with a spear, just chop the thing into kindling. Let's do it.'

The Free State warriors linked shields and churned forward through the beach sand, broadswords held above shields and axes raised high, ready to strike.

Just before they came crashing together Nathaniel brought down a bolt of lightning that smashed into the front ranks of the raiders, blowing six of them into smoking pieces of armor and body parts. However, the effort caused the Marine to stumble as the power drained from him, and Tad and another warrior had to slow down to support him before he fell.

But the thunderbolt had done its job, sundering the ranks of the raiders, and allowing The Ten to breach their shield wall and get in amongst them. And this is where The Ten were at their most deadly, with broadswords swinging and axes singing they clove the enemy asunder.

Tad ducked and rolled and stabbed upwards, sliding his knives and short swords under enemy armor, the rest of The Ten parried spear and sword and counterattacked.

But The Forever Man fought in the only way that he knew how. In a style that he had developed in Pictish times when he first fought the Roman legions, and then he had honed it against the Orcs and goblins. He fought like a berserker, with little or no thought for his own safety. His terrible axe never stopped moving. If it did happen to hang up in someone's armor or ribs, he would simply kick the person off and swing again. Always attacking, never defending. All that came within reach of those dazzling steel blades fell as chaff before the storm.

And the raiders lost heart and retreated because they knew that Death walked amongst them.

Eventually the last surviving raiders could retreat no more. They had come to the sea and already stood knee deep in the surging surf.

'Stop,' bellowed Nathaniel. 'Ten to me.'

His warriors rallied about him, forming up into a shield wall. Some were too badly cut or wounded to stand straight, and they leant on their broadswords or axe handles. Two particularly wounded warriors leant against each other, each keeping the other upright, their armor slick with blood that was both others and their own.

But not one lay on the sand. Not one had fallen. And Nathaniel felt his heart swell with pride. For these were men of men. And their fathers were men before them.

'Surrender,' commanded Nathaniel. 'Surrender and we shall give quarter.'

There were some twenty raiders left. All of them had been severely wounded. Their spears were spent, their golden shields had been sundered, and their swords bent and notched.

'Don't be stupid,' continued the king. 'Why fight to the death when there is no need to. You cannot stand against us, to continue to do so is suicide.'

One by one the raiders dropped their weapons into the sea and stepped forward out of the surf. Then they came to stand before Nathaniel, and at the command of one who appeared to be in charge, they knelt.

'We surrender,' the one in charge said. 'And, on behalf of my men, I, Carrig Faolan O'Niall, ask that you carry out your punishment on me alone. I am their leader, and thus I am the one who should pay.'

'Well,' answered Nathaniel. 'We shall see. But first things first, Carrig, we need to talk. You and your men come with us and I shall do my best to stop the townsfolk lynching you all. After what you lot did to Portavaddie, you aren't very popular around here.'

'If it makes any difference,' said Carrig. 'That wasn't us. It was the Marquess of Donegall and his men.'

'Whatever,' said Nathaniel. 'Same old same old. You're the enemy and they will want to string you up or worse.'

As if to prove Nathaniel's point, a crowd of armed civilians came trotting over the small hill and onto the beach. They were being led by a short rotund man wearing a garish red gown of office and carrying a broadsword that looked about a foot too long for him and a few pounds too heavy.

'Greetings,' he puffed to the Marine. 'We, the people of Port Stanraer give our thanks for your timely intervention. We were, of course, prepared to defend ourselves but you gentlemen did a sterling job indeed. We would like to invite you back to the town hall. Our doctors will see to your wounds and drink and food shall be provided. I may even manage to convince the town treasurer to forward you all a stipend of some sort to show the depth of our appreciation. Now, however, I think that you should hand over the prisoners to us so that we might take care of them.'

'You mean, string them up,' said Nathaniel.

'That would seem to be the appropriate thing,' answered the rotund man. 'Now come along, gentlemen,' he continued. 'Let us not allow things to lead to any unpleasantness, after all, you and your men are exhausted, and many are wounded, you could hardly afford to get into another fight, could you?' The man smiled, a false showing of teeth stretched across his chubby face.

Nathaniel stared at the official for a few seconds then he turned to the little big man. 'Tad.'

'Yes, sire?'

'Sort this moron out, will you.'

'Straight away, my king,' said Tad as he stepped forward and kicked the official in the knee. The chubby man fell forward, and as he did so, he met Tad's fist coming the other way. The sound of his jaw breaking was audible to all as he fell, unconscious, onto the sand.

Tad puffed his chest out and took a deep breath. 'Ladies and gentlemen of Port Stanraer,' he shouted. 'May I present to you, The Forever Man, Marine Master Sergeant Nathaniel Arnthor Hogan, King of the Free State, leader of the Picts, wielder of the axe, and savior of the town of Port Stanraer.'

'Steady on, old man,' whispered Nathaniel. 'You'll make me blush.'

Tad grinned.

The crowd that had followed the short rotund official down to the beach all knelt in supplication to their king.

Then one spoke out. 'Apologies, my king,' he said. 'We had no idea it was you. We've never actually seen you before. In fact, some weren't even sure if you existed.'

'Well, at least we can put a stop to that particular argument then,' said Nathaniel. 'I definitely exist. Now, what's your name?'

The man stood up. 'Duncan Manning, sire. I'm the blacksmith.'

'Well, Duncan Manning. Who was that?' asked Nathaniel, pointing at the prostrate fat man.

'That was Alderman Thomas, sire. Town leader.'

'Not anymore,' said Nathaniel. 'He is now Thomas the town fool and you, Duncan Manning, are the town alderman with all duties and privileges that go with that position.'

The man bowed. 'Thank you, my king. I won't let you down.'

'Good. Now, your first official duty is to take us to the town inn, bring doctors to treat all of the wounded, and that includes the raiders, and provide us all with food and drink. Your second duty is to organize someone to take care of the town fool. See that he doesn't choke to death on his own blood or something. Okay?'

The new alderman nodded and turned to immediately start giving orders. Another man approached Nathaniel. 'Please follow me, sire,' he said. 'I shall show all to the inn.'

***

Nathaniel took another swig of mead, held it in his mouth for a second and then swallowed. 'Good stuff this,' he said as he held his mug up for more.

A young woman scuttled over with a jug and refilled for him, curtsying frantically as she did so.

'So, Carrig,' said Nathaniel. 'Talk to me. Tell me, am I correct in assuming that you lot come from Ireland?'

Carrig nodded his affirmation.

'So,' continued the Marine. 'Why the raiding? Seems a bloody inefficient way to collect goods and supplies. I mean, you've got the whole of Ireland to scavenge from, and if your rate of attrition was similar to ours, then there must be more than enough of everything to go around.'

Carrig looked ill at ease. Uncomfortable with what he was about to say. Eventually he simply took a deep breath and started. 'Initially, sire, there was enough to go around. And more than enough. In the first year I'd say that we lost close to 90 percent of the population. Maybe even a little more. But those who survived began to claw their way back. After the initial waves of lawlessness, people like the Marquess of Donegall, men who were used to power and comfortable with leading, banded people together. Stamped out violent crime and started farming collectives. Times were harsh, but no one starved, and crime became virtually nonexistent. And then …'

Carrig paused and his eyes took on a hunted look, darting from side to side as if, even the thought of what he was about to talk about filled him with fear. Or perhaps not fear, more like, trepidation.

'Carry on, man,' prompted Nathaniel. 'I need to know.'

'Do you know the standing stones at Carroareagh?' questioned Carrig.

'No,' responded Nathaniel. 'Why, is it important?'

Carrig shrugged. 'It gives a geographical point to the story but never mind. The thing is, some ten years after the pulse-light something started to happen around the stone circle at Carroareagh.' Again Carrig hesitated.

'Carry on,' insisted Nathaniel. 'And be not embarrassed if what you are about to reveal seems less than believable. I can assure you, since the pulse we have all experienced our share of the bizarre.'

'It's not that,' continued Carrig. 'It's simply so hard to explain. You see, we started getting reports of disturbances. Strange happenings. People murdering their entire families. Mothers setting their children to flame and laughing whilst they did so. Fathers raping daughters, brothers killing sisters, cows attacking other cows and feasting on their flesh. Stories of absolute horror and bedlam.'

The Irishman paused while he took a drink of mead. Nathaniel noticed that the warrior's hand shook slightly, such was the strength of his emotions that the telling of his story evoked.

'The marquess commanded a group of twenty warriors to investigate. I was one of them. Bear in mind, this was some twelve years ago so I was still a junior, not an officer like I am today. We traveled on horseback to the area of Carroareagh and we were but a mile from the standing stones themselves when we first saw evidence. Whole villages burned to the ground. Bodies torn limb from limb.

'That late afternoon we came across the first survivor. A woman, late forties I would guess. She stood in the middle of a small village, totally naked. Covered in blood and excrement. Her eyes …'

Carrig shuddered. 'Her eyes were like windows into hell. As soon as she saw us, she attacked. Like a ravening beast, she was. Her strength was such that she pulled our captain's horse to the ground, and before we could intervene, she had ripped his head from his shoulders. We ran her through with our lances but even then, she took a while to die, all the time screaming and cursing us.

'We wrapped the captain's body and head in blankets and strapped him to his horse, then we continued in the direction of the stones. After another few minutes of riding we saw them.

'Not human nor animal were they. Although their basic shape was humanoid. More shadow than flesh, they stood as high as a man, but they were almost transparent. And thin as a wraith. The only part of them that was easy to see were their teeth. Their mouths unusually large and full of shark-like rows of canines.

'But that was not what made them so dangerous. No. It was their ability to enter the human mind and instantly drive from it any semblance of goodness or sanity. As soon as we saw them we experienced waves of debilitating nausea and then, almost as one, we turned on each other. Friend against friend, brother against brother, soldier against officer.

'Someone struck me on the head and I passed out. When I awoke, the sun had gone down and night had fallen. Around me lay the corpses of my compatriots. Everyone was dead. I can only assume that they had ignored me, mistaking my unconscious form as death. Even the horses had experienced the terrible madness that had overcome us all. They had turned on each other, kicking and biting and killing.'

Carrig shook his head, as if trying to drive the memories from his mind.

'I walked home. It took me three days, and when I finally got there and reported to the marquess, he did not believe me. The next day he sent another detachment out. Not one returned.'

Nathaniel stood up and fetched a jug of mead, filling Carrig's mug before he sat down again.

'There was nothing that we could do against them. They came to be called The Desolaters, and over the coming years they spread like the vilest of cancers, eating up both the land and the people. They took the whole of Ireland from the lake Lough Neagh southwards. And we were forced onto the northeastern coastlines from Ballycastle to Kilkeel.'

'How is it that any of you have survived?' asked Nathaniel.

'At first we ran. We hid. But then we decided that it was fight or die. After time we learned. They fear flame. They burn like kindling. They can be cut with sharp steel. But, most importantly, a wall of gold weakens their Desolation powers. Presented with a golden shield wall their power is lessened to such an extent that a well-trained and determined group of warriors can get in amongst them. In fact, to fight without the protection of gold would be madness.

'That left us with only two problems; firstly, there is only a very limited amount of gold and, secondly, even with that advantage, they are incredibly hard to defeat. Now we keep our small strip of coastline and they control the rest of my beloved Ireland. So, over time we decided to form raiding parties and pillage like the Vikings of old. We had little other choice given the lack of mineral resources and such left available to us.'

'For God's sake,' exclaimed Nathaniel. 'Why did you not simply send a delegation asking for help? Or why didn't you simply leave Ireland?'

Carrig smiled wryly. 'Actually, we did try. Some eight years ago. We sent two ice skimmers out. Neither came back. It took us a couple more years to perfect our designs and then we sent another two. One in this direction and one further up the coast, the other side of Hadrian's Wall. That one came back. And they had the direst of tales to tell. They claim that they were attacked by creatures that could only be described as Orcs. Grey-skinned, well-armed and ferocious in combat. They saw no sign of any human beings. We decided that the United Kingdom had experienced a similar fate to our own and had been taken over by alien creatures. It was only after a few more years, when we started to become really desperate, that we began to send explorers out once again. The raids are the results of that.'

Carrig took a deep breath. 'If it counts for anything … I am sorry. Men do strange things in desperate times.'

'A sad story well told,' said Nathaniel. 'Nevertheless, something has to be done about this. Tomorrow two thousand of my cavalry will be arriving. I will select one hundred and seventy men to accompany The Ten and I and we shall set forth to see this marquess of yours. I think that we need to talk. You shall come with and I need you to select one of each of your men to be in each boat. I have no time to train my men in their use. I want you to know, Carrig, that this is a peaceful mission. I simply want to bring an end to the raids and I see no reason why we need to go to war. As the last of very few humans left we should all work together.'

'I agree,' said Carrig. 'Unfortunately, you will find the marquess is rather a strange man. Obsessed with his rank and power. I am not sure how he will react.'

'Carrig,' continued Nathaniel. 'Never mistake my friendly attitude for one of weakness. If the marquess defies me then I shall destroy him and his people, your people, utterly and without mercy. You saw how easily a mere handful of us defeated almost two hundred of your best. Imagine what two thousand can achieve. He will listen to reason or he shall be cut down.'

The Irishman nodded. 'Sire,' he said. 'May I ask a question now?'

Nathaniel nodded.

'When your men attacked us … that lightning bolt …?'

The Marine nodded.

'How?' asked Carrig.

Without saying anything Nathaniel held out his empty hand, palm up. And then a ball of incandescent fire appeared above it, the heat so hot that all around had to pull back.

Carrig went pale.

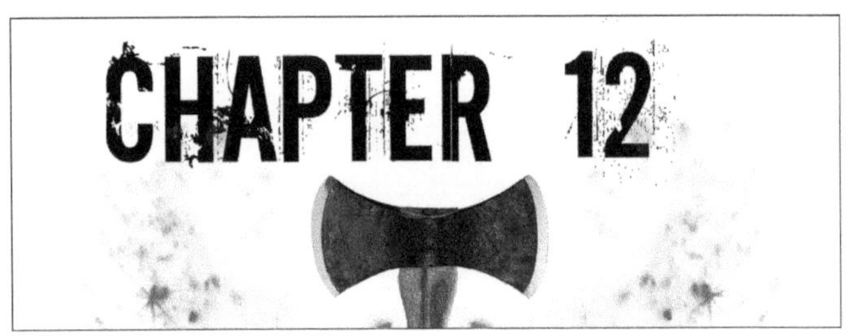

CHAPTER 12

Orc Sergeant Kob was in the Free State. As it happened, he had found it fairly simple to enter.

After a few days of studying the actual wall from a distance, he had concluded that there was no way through it or over it. So that left the choice of under or around. He had chosen around.

Then he had simply waited until spring tide, waded out into the ice-choked sea, and walked around the wall. It hadn't been easy, but Orcs were tough and almost impervious to the cold, so he had made it.

Also, he was confident that he could achieve the same infiltration with a small group. Maybe four or five, no more. Of course, he was now stuck inside the Free State for two weeks, until the next spring tide, but that didn't bother him. He had a lot of work to do.

Kob spent the following two weeks working mainly at night. Hiding in the day. Using the vast forests and the mountain grottos to secrete himself during the daylight hours and then scouting, carefully and thoroughly for the rest of the time.

He made detailed maps, took note of any major, and even many minor, happenings. He noted who lived where and guesstimated the sizes and importance of any villages and military depots that he came across.

All in all, he did a very un-Orclike reconnaissance, showing deep insight and a natural grasp of both politics and tactics.

And then, after two weeks, at the depth of the next spring tide, he ghosted back through the icy seas and headed back to his Fair-Folk masters to impart his newfound knowledge.

***

The young man was officially named Michael Campbell Junior Junior. His father was Michael Campbell Junior and his grandfather was simply Michael Campbell.

But all called him JJ. His father was Junior, and the grandfather was Mister Campbell to all.

JJ had been born three years before the pulse into a family that owned a chain of motor garages that had been in the family since 1901 when there were only nine hundred cars on the roads and the bulk of their work was done on agricultural motors. As a result, the family had lost, overnight, almost one hundred and fifty years of tradition and knowledge.

Undeterred, the Campbell family, particularly Junior and Mister, decided to specialize in the next big thing. And they decided that the next big thing would be the ability to hunt and gather food. As a result, the three Campbell males were now counted as the best fieldsmen in the Free State. Their hunting skills were second to none, and between the three of them, they could name, find, and cook, or utilize in some fashion, just about any wild spice or food-type that grew.

Like many professional outdoorsmen they were taciturn by nature, hardworking, tough, and honest. It was widely accepted that a Campbell's word was his bond.

But, as JJ stared at what he saw in front of him the first thing that came to his mind was—there is no way that anyone is going to believe me.

He had been hunting for venison, and as was often his custom, he had ventured on the other side of the wall. Some species of game were more plentiful on the Fair-Folk side and thus easier to hunt. He had been tracking a large roe deer when he had come across a set of tracks that he had never seen. They were similar to bird tracks but were far too large. Human child sized. Also, the animal was too heavy to be any member of the avian family that he had ever seen before. He had heard tales of African ostriches weighing in at almost three-hundred pounds but the largest bird that he had ever come across was the great bustard at almost four foot tall and weighing eighty pounds.

Whatever this bird was, JJ figured it to weigh about a hundred pounds and stand at four or five feet in height, judging from the length of its stride.

Regardless, he had followed the lone set of tracks, keeping under cover, and ensuring that he walked slowly and silently.

After twenty minutes of tracking he had come across the rest of them.

They were not birds. They were not people. They were … bird-people?

JJ watched them from the shadows. It was a group of six. They appeared to be adult males, between four and five foot in height. Humanoid in appearance, clawed bird-like feet, normal arms with taloned fingers. He noted that, unlike humans, they had only two fingers and a thumb.

They were painfully thin, but that appeared to be by design and not due to starvation. Their musculature showed like steel cables under their skin and there was not an ounce of body fat. Likewise, their bones appeared to be much finer than a human.

Their faces were small and triangular in shape. They did not have beaks, as such, but their jaws did protrude forward, and their teeth were a row of needle sharp fangs.

But the thing that made them stand out the most was their wings. At least ten feet in span, they looked exactly like a bats'. In fact, the more that JJ studied the creatures the more bat-like he found them. In his mind he christened them bat-people.

They were sitting around a fire and were clad only in rough spun loincloths. Several small game animals, rabbits, and pigeon were spitted over the flames and the bat-people squatted close to the warmth, their wings wrapped around their torsos when they were at rest. Like cocoons of finest leather.

They were communicating via a series of chirps and low whistles. Almost birdlike in quality but less musical. JJ was about to slip away when he realized that he could understand what they were saying. Not in any detail, but the general gist of the conversation.

They were happy that game was plentiful. They found the weather to be colder than they were used to. There were many more of them scattered about the forest. They had no idea where they were in either time or space.

And finally, they were more than relieved at having escaped the enemy. When JJ heard, or more closely, perceived, the mention of an enemy, he paid closer attention. However, he could glean little more from his rudimentary understanding of their conversations apart from; the enemy was ruthless, plentiful and was referred to as either The Enemy or the Annihilators.

After a while he also learned that the bat-people called themselves Vandals. Not wanting to take any chance of being discovered, JJ slipped backwards into the trees and left, heading back to the wall and the Free State, away to tell his father what he had seen.

***

Time does not run in a linear fashion. That particular concept is a man-made concept governed by our ego and our desperate need to quantify and control. Man has come up with concepts of time ranging from time-as-a-forth-dimension, through to the unbelievably complicated concepts of super-string theory and time-as-an-eleven-dimensional-construct. But all of these theories are simply mankind attempting to bottle time and eke it out in understandable, controllable increments. We may as well try to bottle a thunderstorm.

Time is unquantifiable. It happens all at once. Everything that has ever happened, that ever will happen and that ever might happen, is all taking place at the exact same concurrent time. To affect the past will affect the future and, conversely, to affect the future will affect the past.

Thus, the Unicorn stood in the center of the confluence of ley lines next to the standing stones circle of Stonehenge and sorted through the nodes of time around it. Slicing parcels of it into usable sizes and extrapolating them into possible outcomes and effects.

The Forever Man was in danger. He was always in danger. But, at the moment, it was not the correct time for the Unicorn to help. It was too early.

And time spooled out in all directions at once, bringing with it the beginning and the end of all that we shall ever know.

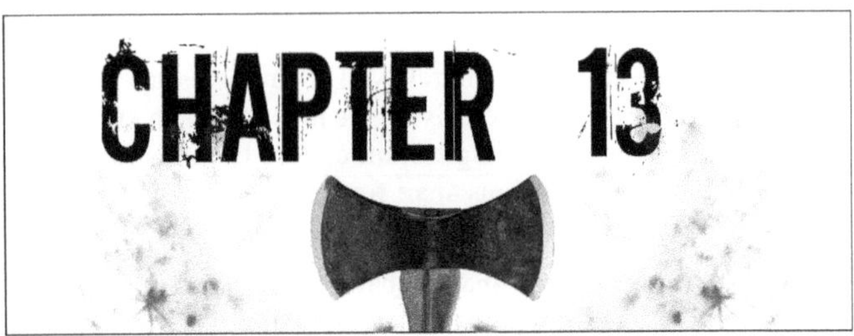

CHAPTER 13

General Carson had stayed behind to control the defense of the wall. However, he had sent his 2IC, Colonel Bricksmith, with the two thousand cavalry that had been dispatched to protect the northwest shores from the raiders.

Nathaniel had spent a day and a night with the colonel, firstly handpicking one hundred and eighty soldiers to accompany him across the sea to Ireland, and secondly, in creating a plan to disperse the rest of the eighteen hundred cavalry into defensive positions along the coast.

The Marine was fairly confident that there were no raids planned for the immediate future and Carrig had confirmed this. However, he and the colonel had split the cavalry into ten equal groups of around two hundred each and sent them off, traveling up and down the coast from Kirkcudbright in the south, to Ardrossan in the north.

Their mission was twofold; first they were to see if there were any raiders or if any had ever struck. Then they were to provide protection and help set up a system of town and village guards. Secondly, they were to spread word and story of the king and how he had exacted vengeance for the raid on Portavaddie. For it struck Nathaniel that, although he was king and leader of the Free State, many people knew of him only by rumor or hearsay. The cavalry was there to harden the dust of rumor into the solid stone of truth.

After two days, Nathaniel, Tad, The Ten, and the selected soldiers were ready to travel across the seas. Each of the ice boats were piloted by one of the survivors of Carrig's raiding party.

Some of the raiders had refused to work for the Marine, and in a show that had shocked many of them; Nathaniel had accepted their refusals and then had them put to death by the sword. Tad, who knew the Marine better than anyone, saw how deeply this act of savagery affected him—but he also knew that hard times oft called for harsh measures, so he said nothing in argument.

Since then not one had answered back to him, nor his men.

Now, thirty fully laden iceboats skimmed across the packed slush of the Irish Sea, carrying with them almost two hundred of the Free State's finest warriors. They had set out at sunrise, the emerging sun frosting the ragged ice sea with a wash of pink and silver. The ever-present pulse light above scored the wash with careless streaks of random color and seagulls swooped and dove about them, seeking scraps of anything edible.

Shortly, the flotilla cruised into the mists and all around became a silver fog. Vision limited to forty yards.

Carrig took out a small brass compass and set it on the bow. The needle moved from point to point, stopping every now and then to stay on due south.

'Does that thing work?' asked Tad.

Carrig nodded. 'The pulse light affects it, but only slightly. One has to keep an eye on it and steer using a mean average. It's not pinpoint but it will get us close enough. Once we get closer to land the mists rise and we can see where we are going once again.'

Carrig said that the trip would take eight hours. After the first few hours Nathaniel slipped into a half sleep. The continual silver gray all about him and the white noise of the hull sliding over the ice and the slush lulled him into a state of meditation, and as he sat without talking nor moving, he moved slowly through the five states from the gross level, through subtle, bliss and I-ness, and into the final level known as objectless or Asamprajnata.

Tall they stood. Perhaps eight foot high. Their bodies were enclosed in a strange armor. Chitinous. Insect-like. Their legs bent backwards at the knees and their feet were more akin to claws. Two sets of arms. One pair ending in a multi-digit taloned hand, the other pair each ended in a three-foot blade made from the same material as the armor.

They drew closer and he felt fear. He could see them more clearly now. It was not armor, it was an exoskeleton. Part of their body itself. The heads were spiked, and their compound eyes flicked from side-to-side, independent of one another, scanning in all directions at once.

There were many of them. Countless numbers. Too many for him to fight. Before he could turn and run they had him, piercing him with their talons. Cutting him with their bladed appendages. His axe simply bounced off their armored skin.

He screamed in terror …

… he was somewhere else. Floating. All about him an impenetrable golden light. He was safe. The fear had left him, and he realized that the fear had merely been a manifestation of itself. A forewarning. A portend.

'The Annihilators are coming,' it said.

'I know,' he answered. 'I shall be ready when they do.'

'Good. And I shall be here to help you.'

And Nathaniel turned his head and saw it, standing tall and proud. Its hide a blinding white. Its eyes the most crystalline blue. Its horn a blend of all the colors of the pulse-light.

Unicorn.

Tad shook The Forever Man's shoulder.

'Hey, boss,' he said. His voice held low. Quiet. 'Wake up. You dozed off. We're almost there.'

Nathaniel looked around. The sun was low in the sky and the flotilla had emerged from the sea mists and was heading towards the shore, some six hundred yards away. As he looked about, Carrig changed tack slightly, angling the ice boat so that they were traveling almost parallel to the beach.

'We need to get a mile or so north,' he said. 'As I said, our navigation is less than pinpoint accurate. Our village is fairly close though. So, King Nathaniel,' he continued. 'What's the plan when we get there? It's just that, there is every chance that, as we disembark, we may be attacked as soon as the people realize that we're strangers. Well. That most of us are strangers.'

'I'm going to rely on you, good Carrig,' answered Nathaniel. 'As soon as we beach I want you front and center, yelling out that we come in peace. Also, I want you waving this above your head for all that its worth.' Nathaniel held up a spear that Tad had tied a white sheet to. 'Then we will all stand, weapons sheathed and try our best to look nonthreatening.'

'If they do still attack?' enquired Carrig.

'Make sure that they don't,' warned The Forever Man. 'For if they do I shall decimate your people and leave what is left to the Desolaters.'

Carrig blanched. 'I will do my best, sire.' 'See that you do.'

The small flotilla beat before the wind for another twenty minutes before the village hove into view. Carrig jibed the ice boat about and the flotilla followed. Within minutes they were grinding up onto the sandy shore.

Carrig leapt off the boat and ran up onto the beach waving his white flag of truce above his head.

Nathaniel's men also disembarked with haste and formed up in ranks behind the flag waving Irishman. The Marine strode up the beach to stand next to Carrig, as did Tad.

They all stood still and waited. It didn't take at all long before people started to appear. Firstly, a mix of villagers. Wide-eyed children, bold young boys, old men, and housewives. Some carried weapons of a sort but most simply carried the tools of their trades. Brooms, spades, baskets, and sundry items.

Not long after the crowd started to form, a detachment of soldiers marched into view. At a guess, Nathaniel put their number at three hundred or so. Riding at the head of the column, on a small but healthy-looking pony, carrying a short whip, was a man that Carrig immediately pointed out as the Marquess of Donegall.

The man rode his pony directly up to Nathaniel and peered down at him.

'Where are my men?' he demanded.

'Dead,' replied Nathaniel. 'Apart from the few that you see standing in front of you.'

'You dare to kill my men?'

'You dare to raid my country?' retaliated The Forever Man.

The marquess raised his hand above his head in an obvious preplanned command and his soldiers fanned out, forming a shield wall one hundred long and three deep. The movement was carried out smoothly and with great precision. Nathaniel was impressed.

'I am under a flag of truce,' he pointed out to the marquess.

'But I am not,' retorted the Irishman.

Carrig stepped forward. 'My lord,' he said. 'If I may. King Nathaniel comes to negotiate, not to fight. I strongly advise that you accept his treaty and listen to him.'

The marquess edged his pony closer to Carrig, almost touching him. 'You advise me? You sniveling little turd. You come back here having lost and entire raiding party and then you seek to beg my forgiveness and advise me to seek treaty with this ersatz king.' The marquess lashed out with his whip, cutting Carrig across the cheek and bringing forth a welter of bright red blood.

Carrig did not flinch. 'My lord,' he continued. 'I accept responsibility for the loss of our men. However, do not attack these people. I could not bear to see the loss of more of our people. We are spread too thin as it is.'

The marquess sneered at Nathaniel. 'We outnumber you almost two to one,' he said. 'I shall give you five minutes to surrender your arms.'

'Don't need five minutes,' said Nathaniel. 'Just hang fire for a few seconds while I ask Carrig something.'

The marquess nodded, confident in his superior numbers.

'Hey, Carrig,' called Nathaniel. 'How would you like to be the marquess?'

Carrig shook his head. 'Not much, sire. Happy in the position that I am.'

'Well, tough titty,' responded the Marine. 'I'm afraid that you don't have a choice. You're the new marquess. Well done. All praise, and so on.'

'You can't simply make him a marquess, you stupid idiot,' blustered the man on the pony.

'Just have,' said Nathaniel.

'I take it that this charade means that you offer your surrender?'

'Yes,' agreed The Forever Man. 'But not to you. I surrender myself and my troops to Carrig Faolan O'Niall, the true Marquess of Donegall.' Nathaniel turned to his warriors, held his hand high and bellowed out. 'All hail, Carrig Faolan O'Niall, the true Marquess of Donegall.'

As one his men shouted back. 'All hail marquess Carrig of Donegall.'

Nathaniel glanced over to take a look at the Irishmen lined up in a shield wall along the top of the beach and he could see sighs of confusion and bemusement. He walked over to Carrig and knelt before him.

'Carrig O'Niall,' he shouted out. 'I, Marine Master Sergeant Nathaniel Hogan, also known as King Arnthor of the Picts, leader of the Free State of Scotland, and The Forever Man, do put myself and my warriors under your command. All hail, true Marquess of Donegall.'

And then The Forever Man stood up, pulled in the Earth power around him and unleashed a fireball of massive proportions into the sky. It crackled upwards until it looked like another sun in the sky. Then it exploded with the sound of a thousand fireworks. Pieces of flaming plasma fizzed through the air as they fell to the ground, setting alight trees and grass as they touched down.

The ex-marquess's pony reared up in terror, throwing its rider to the ground and bolting.

Carrig made a decision, strode over, and picked the ex-marquess up by his shirtfront, snatching his whip from his hand as he did so. 'Now listen to me, you pompous turd,' he snarled. 'Believe me when I tell you that attacking these men would result in our annihilation. That is no aspersion to our bravery or competence, they are simply better soldiers than us and they have The Forever Man with them. I am sorry, I didn't want to be made the marquess, but you left no other choice. You idiot.'

Then Carrig turned to face the massed Irish troops. 'Hear me,' he shouted. 'These men come in peace. They come under a flag of truce to parley and not to do battle. The ex-marquess has dishonored them and us by ignoring the flag of truce.' Carrig pointed at two men standing in the van of the shield wall. 'You, Scott, and you, Travis. The ex-marquess is under arrest. Put him in chains and place him in the town jail. He shall be dealt with in due course.'

The two men hesitated, not sure whom to listen to but Carrig trucked no hesitation. 'Come on,' he shouted. 'Move it.'

Scott and Travis jogged forward and grabbed an arm each, bodily dragging the protesting former leader away.

Nathaniel approached Carrig and praised him. 'Well done.'

'I feel like a traitor,' responded the Irishman.

The Marine shook his head. 'No. The old marquess was not the right man for the job. He inspired cruelty in his men, as was apparent in the Portavaddie raid. He ignored a flag of truce, he accused his own men of cowardice before bothering to hear out the fact, and last but definitely not least, your soldiers took the first excuse given them to rebel against him. You are no traitor—you are the new leader.'

Carrig shrugged. 'So, my king, what do you suggest the new leader of the Irish does now?'

'I suggest that we find a place to encamp my men. We have our own rations and tents, we simply need a level patch of open ground near water. Then you and I can talk.'

Carrig nodded. 'It shall be done.'

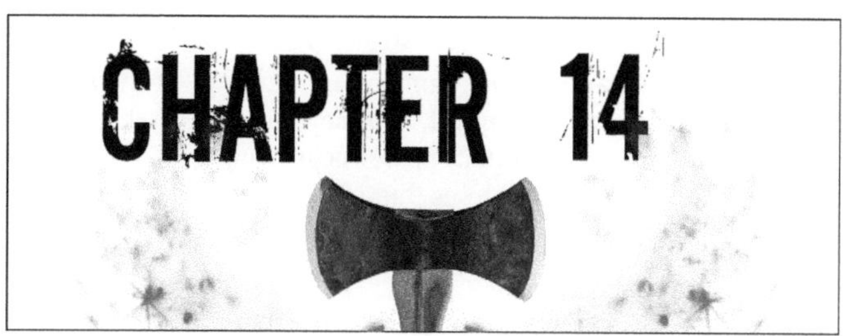

CHAPTER 14

'The rumors are spreading,' said Seth. 'Of that, there is no doubt.'

'The problem is,' added Ammon. 'If we strenuously deny the existence of The Free State it will only strengthen the humans need to seek the truth.'

The rest of the council of twelve sat without talking. The commander and the chief mage had summoned them, and as custom dictated, they would only talk or advise when called upon to do so.

'As we know,' continued Ammon. 'The humans are malleable to a certain point. As long as we continue to be perceived as their only hope for continued existence, if not prosperity, then we can control them. But this Free State furnishes them with hope. Hope that they can survive on their own, without our leadership and guiding hand. Without our rules and laws. And it goes without saying that we have found the human to be a very truculent being if he is given room to think. Even now there has been a spate of recent sabotage that has severely weakened our economy. Nothing that we cannot recover from but still very irksome. I am less than pleased.

Also, I have received a very succinct report on the Free State from Orc Sergeant Kob who penetrated their defenses and spent a fortnight behind the wall, cataloging the human behavior that he observed there.'

There was a slight frisson in the air at the mention of Orc Sergeant Kob's name. Ammon picked it up but said nothing. He knew that the Fair-Folk were worried about this strange Orc that thought for himself and was capable of carrying out missions that involved both subtlety and invention. But he also knew that Kob was a one-off. An aberration. As such he did not merit worry. After all, Ammon observed, it was not as if they were suddenly going to become swamped with proactive, ambitious Orcs. The entire concept was ludicrous.

'According to Sergeant Kob the humans are thriving. Crime is nonexistent, food supplies are plentiful, and they appear to be happy and content. As well as this, their military power is growing. Not to a stage where they would be a significant threat to us, but still, they could be a bother. Things need to be done, good folk, and as such, I have convened this meeting. Ideas, please.'

A mage called Agathocles stood up. He was the senior mage in charge of the mines and the manufacture of the birthing eggs and vats for the battle Orcs.

'Commander,' he said. 'I feel compelled to point out that, with the protracted use that we have made of human labor over the past two decades, we have come to rely on them. Our production of the Constructs who used to do our menial tasks has all but ceased. After all, we have found that a sufficiently motivated human is capable of doing three to four times the work of a Construct.'

'Your point being, Agathocles?' asked Ammon.

'My point, Commander, is that, without human labor it would take us up to ten years or more to replenish our stocks of Constructs to replace current human input. My point is that we cannot afford to lose human input. They have become … necessary to our continued existence.'

Ammon glanced at Seth for confirmation.

The chief mage nodded. 'What Agathocles says is correct, Commander,' he concurred. 'The humans farm our crops, catch our fish, weave our clothes, and convert their old buildings to suit us. They carry our messages, clean our dwellings, and generally, assist in almost every aspect of our lives and our comfort.'

'So, what does the council suggest?' asked the commander.

'We advise a complete change in our human governing practices. We need a serious clampdown.'

'Some would say that we have clamped down enough and that is part of the problem,' argued Ammon.

'No,' disagreed Seth. 'We have discussed the problem and feel that we have, perhaps, been approaching it all from the wrong angle. At the moment we subjugate through laws that result, on the whole, in either corporal or capital punishment of some sort. That can be either physical punishment or ostracization or both. But we are still using our laws to bend the human will to our way of thinking. Instead, we need to start changing the way that they, the humans, actually think.'

'A bold statement, senior mage,' countered Ammon. 'How?'

'Separate development together,' stated Seth. 'We need to control their schooling, rewrite their history and their lessons, favoring our intervention more.

'We already limit Orc and goblin interaction with the humans, but we must become even stricter with that. However, we temper it by giving them "Free Areas". Areas that are solely human, except, of course, for a few necessary Orc guards.

'We allow them some free trade amongst each other. Trade unrestricted by our quotas but in very limited amounts.

'We elevate the current worthy humans to an even higher state, showing what magnanimous leaders we are. Perhaps we institute a worthy human day, declare a public holiday of feasting to replace some of their current festival days.

'You see, we need to give them the feeling of freedom whilst, at the same time, subjugating them utterly. Those who already consider themselves free will have no reason to search for a mythical Free State.'

Ammon nodded his approval. 'As I said before, Seth, bold. But it makes sense. I approve. Put together a formal proposal so that we might start on this sweeping plan of yours. Now, lastly, before we go. Good council members, I need you to bend your minds to another problem. After Sergeant Kob's report one fact has become painfully aware to me. That fact is that the human Free State is being held together, in the main, by a single human. One who goes by the name of Nathaniel Hogan. He is an ex-military sergeant that has assumed the role of leader of the Free State. There are rumors that he is the self-same human that released such devastating magikal forces against us during the battle of Hadrian's Wall a couple of years back. Personally, I am not sure about that. Senior mage Seth Hil Nu is more convinced that our magikal opponent is an old lady that lives with a tribe of gypsies. Be that as it may, we need to think of a way to nullify this leader. Something that will not involve full-scale war. Something subtle. Think about it, good folk. Report to Seth. That is all.'

The council stood and bowed as they filed out, leaving the Fair-Folk commander alone.

***

There were six of them, including the twins, Donny and Lonny, ex-SBS soldier Jack Olsen, and three people from Axel's abbey. Paul Jansen, Patrick Smith, and Betty Parker.

At first, Jack had been a little reticent about Axel assigning Betty to their small elite group, but the captain had insisted. And she had proved to be a more than worthy companion. Tough, quiet, and an excellent medic, she pulled her own weight and more.

Over the last couple of months, the two teenage brothers had grown up. Life in the shadows, being constantly on edge and always at war had honed their personalities to an edge. They communicated in short, spare sentences. Their eyes had gained the thousand-yard stare of veterans. But they still joked and laughed. They had lost their innocence but not their humanity.

Jack was the same as he had ever been. Sharp-witted, dry, and unforgiving. The other new boys, Paul and Patrick, had been born pre-pulse but were only in their mid-twenties. Both at the peak of physical fitness. Jack was in no doubt that, had they been his age, they would both have qualified for either the SAS or SBS. Together, the six of them were a formidable team.

The day before, they had flooded a chine clay mine in Cornwall. The clay was essential for making the birthing and development pods and baths for the Orcs, and any disruption to clay production was high on Jack's list.

The mines were worked by humans, so any sabotage had to take place at night so as not to do any physical harm to the laborers.

Flooding a pit mine back in the old days of explosives and electronic detonators would have been a relatively simple task. Nowadays, however, it took a lot more patience and skill.

Fortunately, clay mining uses an inordinate amount of water, so vast dams had been built above the level of the pits to provide water under pressure to turn the clay into a slurry ready for transportation to the drying troughs. The team had spent the week before sawing all of the retaining logs for the dam walls half way through. Working in the pitch-black of night with wood saws and copious quantities of oil to deaden the sound of sawing. On the seventh night they had sneaked a team of dray horses from the stables, killing both Orc guards as they did so. Then they had attached ropes to the weakened timbers and used the horses to simply pull the dam walls down.

The results had been spectacular. Millions of tons of water had cascaded into the open pits, smashing the troughs and gangways and ladders, and filling the pits to the top, rendering them useless for the foreseeable future.

The team had followed up by burning the stables and releasing all of the horses into the wild.

They probably could have killed more Orcs if they had burned down the barracks. Especially if they had nailed the main doors shut beforehand.

However, Axel had been very strict on that point. Their job was to sabotage. They were to keep loss of life to a minimum. They were treading a fine line. They wanted to create maximum disturbance, but not to spur the Fair-Folk into full mobilization.

So they burned, they released cattle, they poisoned wells and then left notes saying that the water was poisoned, forcing the Fair-Folk to have new wells dug. They flooded mines and stole food and weapons. But they kept killing to a minimum. Even though they knew that the same rules would not apply to them in return.

If they were captured it would be the rope. A very public hanging and a shallow grave.

They had been out in the field for almost a month now and Jack was taking them back to the abbey for some well-earned R&R.

Soft beds, hot water, plentiful food, and unlimited quantities of alcohol.

And then, after a week of rest, they would be back on the road again. Doing what they did best.

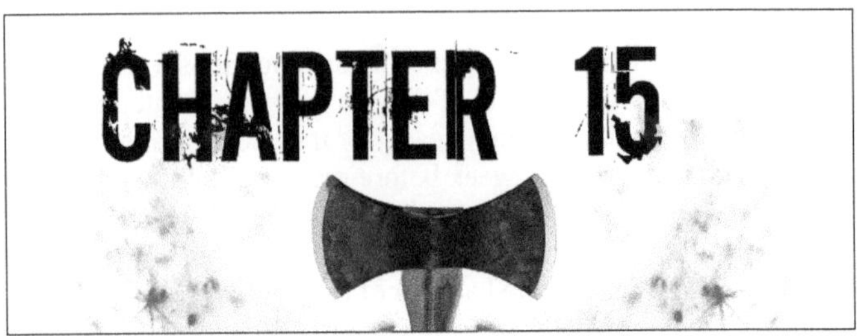

CHAPTER 15

Nathaniel and his troops had set up camp on a flat field next to a large stream that ran strong and clear with ample water. Carrig had provided a small herd of goats that his men had dressed and spitted over a large fire. They had combined this with their own rations to provide a good solid meal for all.

The ex-marquess had been placed in the town jail and Nathaniel and Carrig had spent much of the evening visiting ranking officers and various townsfolk of note explaining the new status quo.

The military men were happy and in agreement, something that convinced Nathaniel that he had made the correct decision.

On the whole, the town noteworthies were also on the same page. One or two voiced concerns and Carrig considered them and allayed them. Two men, the town treasurer and the ex-marquess' cousin, the High Lord O'Shea were both vociferous and threatening in their disagreement, both seeming to believe that, if there was to be a change of leadership, it should fall to them.

Before the evening was out they were both keeping the ex-marquess company.

The next morning Nathaniel, Tad, and The Ten were up before sunrise to meet with Carrig and two of his ranking officers, Colonel Liam Brogan and Colonel Oisin Riely.

It was Carrig's plan to show The Forever Man the enemy.

The Desolaters.

The platoon left the camp on foot. Nathaniel's two hundred men plus another two hundred men under the direct command of Carrig, the new marquess.

Nathaniel, Tad, and Carrig marched in the van of the formation but Nathaniel's men marched at the rear, giving way to the locals with their local experience.

They marched five abreast and the long column of golden shields shone in the rising sunlight like the scales of a many-legged beast of legend. Like England and Scotland, the Irish forests had flourished, and the land was thick with majestic ash, oak, yew, and elm.

Bird life was plentiful, and Nathaniel noticed many massive wild boars flitting through the shadows, their tusks glistening with saliva, skin bristling with short hard tufts of hair.

Tad noticed a track on the side of the trail and broke ranks to look at it.

'Cat?' he questioned Carrig.

'Puma,' answered the Irishman. 'No idea where they came from. There have ever been rumors of brown Puma living in this part of Ireland and it seems as though they were correct. Now many of them roam freely. We lose a lot of sheep and goats to them, but they are canny creatures. Impossible to trap and very difficult to hunt down. The best way to keep them at bay is by using dogs. Lots of dogs.'

At midday the platoon stopped for a quick trail lunch of water and dried rations. Desiccated fruits and leather-hard cured meat. After twenty minutes they were once again on the march.

'Where exactly are we going?' enquired Nathaniel.

'Nowhere specific,' answered Carrig. 'I merely want you to see evidence of the Desolaters. As long as we continue heading in this direction we will come up against them. They will attack, we will drive them off.'

Even as Carrig was talking Nathaniel noticed a subtle change in the atmosphere. It had become quiet. Unnaturally so. No bird song, no susurration of bugs and beetles. Even the wind had dropped, leaving the leaves on the trees still and silent.

Carrig raised his right hand above his head, his fist clenched. The platoon stamped to a halt.

'They're coming,' he said to Nathaniel, his voice rough with suppressed fear. 'Shield wall,' he shouted to his troops. 'Three deep. Move it.' The

Irishmen ran to position, lining up, linking their golden shields, and laying their long spears over the top of them. 'Tell your men to take the left flank,' said Carrig.

Nathaniel nodded and ran to the left. 'Form up on me,' he commanded his warriors. 'Shield wall, two deep on the left flank.'

Although the men of the Free State were primarily cavalry, they had also trained intensively for hand-to-hand combat and they maneuvered into position with grace and purpose.

'Steady men,' shouted out Carrig. 'Keep your shields high. You need to keep gold between them and us at all times. Stab hard and fast. Remember, when they go down they aren't out. Keep stabbing them until they fade away. If the man next to you succumbs to the Desolation and attacks you, do not hesitate to slay him. He is no longer your friend. He has been Desolated and he will destroy you unless you kill him. Good luck, people.'

'This sounds like it's gonna be fun,' mumbled Tad to the Marine.

'Stick with me,' said Nathaniel. 'No way some non-human is going to get the best of me. Hooah!'

'Hooah!' shouted the rest of Nathaniel's men.

And the Desolators attacked. They flowed out of the forest in their hundreds. Wraith-like and shadowy, their maws open impossibly wide to expose row upon row of shark teeth. As they came they screamed, a high-pitched sound that set all on edge and was painful to hear.

Then the Desolation hit them. A wave of unadulterated emotion. Terror, loathing, disgust, and despair all rolled into one gigantic, all-consuming tsunami of bottomless despair and hatred. Hatred of oneself, of the world, of those around you. Of the very air that you were breathing and the light that you saw. Depression.

Two of Nathaniel's men on his right attacked each other. Two friends wordlessly hacking at each other with a fury born of absolute hatred. All down the line men let their shields drop to the floor and tore their hair from their heads, screaming and ululating in terror and horror.

Then the Desolators struck them physically. Their slightness of build and apparent lack of substance was belied by the strength of their blows. They carried no weapons but fought with fist and tooth, bludgeoning soldiers into senselessness, and tearing their throats out with rows of razor-sharp canines.

Nathaniel struggled to clear his mind, fighting against the surfeit of horror and hopelessness that he felt.

'Stop fighting,' said a voice in his head. 'They feed off your fear. Your anger.'

'Who is this?' thought Nathaniel.

'That is not important. Relax your mind. Let their hatred flow around you like a rock in a stream. Do not fight it. Make no attempt to stem the tide. Leave it. Ignore it.'

'Easy for you to say,' said Nathaniel as he swung his axe at a wraith, surprising himself with the solid feel as it struck.

Next to The Forever Man, Tad fought like an automaton. The relatively large size of his golden shield protected him more thoroughly, so he was less affected by the Desolation. He was stepping forward, slipping his shield briefly to one side, stabbing upwards and repeating. All around him Desolaters were falling to the floor and then fading to nothingness as he delivered the coups de grace.

Carrig's men were faring well, they had been exposed to this before and they had kept their shields high and tight. Two or three of them had been taken down by their own men as they turned on each other, and perhaps ten by the Desolators.

Nathaniel's men, however, were not faring well at all. They had not fully appreciated the need to keep the shields high. They had approached the battle in the same way that they would have approached an Orc or goblin or even human opponent. This was different. In fact, fully ten of them had actually slain each other and another twenty had gone down under the ravening of the Desolators.

Nathaniel swung his axe again, fear driving his arm. 'Stop,' repeated the voice. 'Be calm. Think.'

The voice shimmered in The Forever Man's head like a shaft of light. And Nathaniel picked his golden shield up high to protect himself and he obeyed the voice. He purged his mind of anger and retribution. He stood solidly, feet planted securely on the earth. Then he sheathed his axe.

He could still sense the anger and the fear and the horror all around him, but it no longer affected him. It rushed by him like wind over a mountain.

'Good,' encouraged the voice. 'Now, pull in the power of the pulse light. Fill yourself with it.'

Nathaniel did as he was told, drawing in power like a deep breath. Filling his very essence with it.

'Now,' continued the voice. 'Do this …'

A series of complex images flashed through the Marine's mind. A confusing welter of facts and information. He struggled to keep up. To understand what was being imparted to him.

'Stop struggling. You know this. You are The Forever man. This is knowledge that you have always had, that you will always have. I am merely reminding you.'

And then, in an instant, Nathaniel knew that the voice was correct. He knew what to do.

The Forever Man raised his hands high and, with a gesture, unleashed untold power.

Shafts of lightning flashed overhead, crackling across the sky with forks of blue-white fire. Without warning, they started to strike the ground. First singularly and then in increasing numbers. Hundreds and then thousands of individual lightning strikes marched across the field, moving in from behind the Desolators like a rampaging army of heavenly fire.

The ragged bolts of plasma leapt from wraith to wraith and, as each Desolator was touched by the fire, they simply exploded in a welter of flame and smoke, screaming in absolute agony. Fear was an emotion that had never affected them before, but now it overcame them, and they tried, desperately, to escape. But there was nowhere to run. Nowhere to hide. The lightning skittered and scattered across the vast ranks of the Desolators, killing time and time again without pause nor mercy.

The ranks of human soldiers simply stood still and watched, mouths slack and eyes wide with shock and awe.

Black smoke boiled out from the ground around Nathaniel's feet and the air reeked of brimstone.

Then the lightning stopped as abruptly as it had started, and The Forever Man slowly sank to his knees in utter exhaustion. Just before he passed out he saw, in his mind, a fleeting glimpse of a creature of myth and legend.

Blindingly white hide with eyes as deep as oceans and a single horn of coruscating light.

Unicorn.

CHAPTER 16

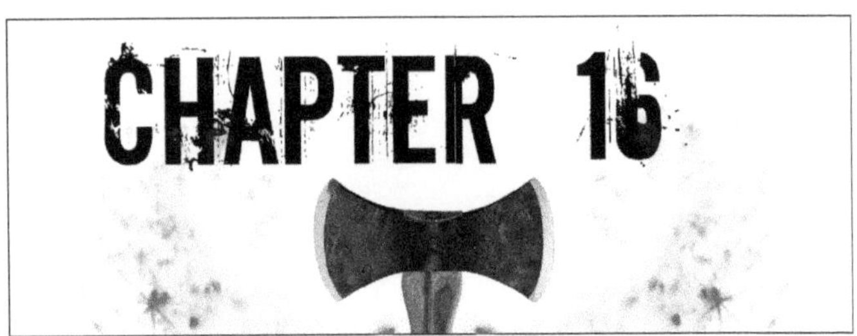

Milly lived by herself in a small thatched cottage that Nathaniel had organized for her. It was close to a stream, had a good fireplace, and Nathaniel had ensured that she always had a ready supply of firewood, food, and water.

In return she helped the local children with their lessons. Although she had received very little formal schooling, being very young when the pulse had struck, she had been involved with figures and bookkeeping when she was a worthy human under the Fair-Folk, in charge of her district. So, she taught figures to the children. Basic math and the practical uses thereof.

She was often alone. But more than that, she was lonely. Although no one actually disliked Milly she was not an easy person to like. Aloof and moody, she was prone to sinking into dark depressions, followed by shiny happy moments of upbeat joyfulness that was impossible to sustain for any length of time.

Most of her idle moments were full of thoughts of Nathaniel. Some of them were merely practical ones, should she bake him a pie? Make him a new jacket? Help him with his admin work?

Other thoughts were less than practical and verged on fantasy. Herself and The Forever Man being married and her being crowned Queen. The names of the children that they would have and the castle that Nathaniel would build for her.

Other thoughts were darker but no less fantastical. What she would do if Nathaniel spurned her? The people that she would kill, the buildings that she would burn. Retribution. But these dark imaginings would fill her with guilt and she would retreat into herself for days on end. Hiding from all.

And the times that Nathaniel was away were the worst. Like now. Once again, he had deserted her. Run away up north to follow some rumor involving bandits from across the sea or such what.

Milly smiled to herself. She wasn't overly worried. He would be back soon, and she would take care of him. She had just finished sewing a new dress. Tissue-thin green cotton, low cut. She would talk to him and cook for him, and finally, she would take him up to his room and they would be one. She could wait. Patience was a virtue that she had spent much time cultivating.

She hummed a song to herself as she cogitated. It was a favorite of Nathaniel's. Milly was too young to know it, but the song was by an old-time band called The Beatles. She didn't know the words or the name of the song, only the melody.

And so, Milly hummed to herself and thought her thoughts of love and abandonment.

"Look out Helter Skelter

She's coming down fast

Yes she is

Yes she is coming down fast"

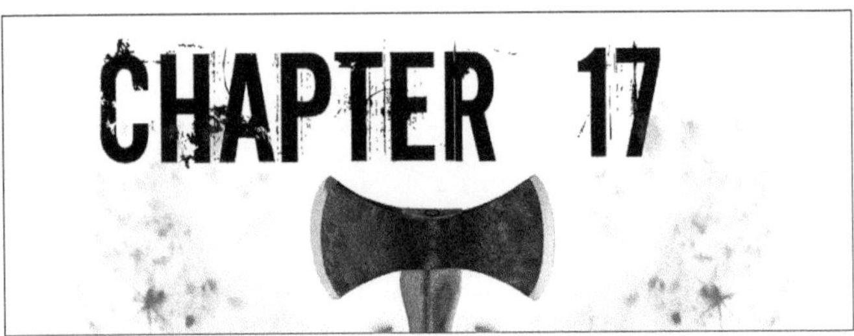

Nathaniel spluttered and shook his head as he sat up, cold water streaming from his face and hair.

'Oh good,' said Tad. 'You're awake.'

'That's freezing,' complained the Marine.

'Yeah well, had to make sure that you woke up. One never knows what's going to happen when you pass out. You could go back to the pixies for all that I know. Best to get you up and about as soon as possible.'

'It doesn't work that way,' said Nathaniel. 'And it's Picts, not pixies.'

'Whatever,' shrugged Tad. 'Didn't want to take any chances.'

The Marine rose slowly and painfully to his feet and looked around. Soldiers were taking care of each other, binding wounds, setting bones. Some more experienced ones were helping to stitch deeper cuts and lacerations. Some simply lay on their backs, resting. Others stood staring blankly. Some laughed. Some talked. Some wept softly over a friend's dead body.

But without exception, whenever any of them looked at The Forever Man it was with an expression of awe and respect.

'I take it we won?' asked Nathaniel.

Tad nodded. 'After you went all Zeus on their asses, they either got burned to a crisp or they ran away. Good result. How did you do that? Never seen you create so much energy at once. Thought that you were going to go supernova and explode.'

The Marine shook his head. 'You wouldn't believe me if I told you.'

'Try me,' insisted Tad.

'A unicorn told me.'

The little big man stood silent for a while before he answered. 'Yep, you're right. I don't believe you. No offence meant.'

'None taken,' assured Nathaniel. 'I hardly believe myself.'

As Nathaniel spoke, Carrig came running over. He dropped to one knee in front of the Marine. 'Sire,' he said. 'You live.'

'Affirmative,' agreed Nathaniel. 'That's me all over. Probably why they call me The Forever Man.'

'With your permission, sire,' asked Carrig. 'I would like to get back to the town as soon as we can move. This story needs to be told. Never before have we had such a great victory. You must have killed many hundreds of them. Perhaps even thousands.'

'Maybe,' said Nathaniel. 'However, I'd be a lot happier if there were a few of their corpses left strewn around the place. Nothing better than a pile of dead bodies to convince a guy that he actually killed something. At the moment, well, all that we can be sure of is that I made them go away. Flame, fire, lightning … poof. Gone. Like a magik trick.'

Carrig got a worried look on his face. 'Never thought of it like that, my lord.'

'Tell you what, Carrig,' said Nathaniel. 'For now, let's say that I killed them. If not, and all that I actually did is piss them off, well then, we'll cross that bridge when we come to it.'

Carrig smiled. 'I'll take that, my lord. I'll take that with great pleasure.'

They all set off as soon as the wounded were stabilized, crutches were cut from the surrounding trees to support those who needed them, and litters constructed to drag the more severely harmed.

It was a slow but triumphant return home, and along the way, Nathaniel told Carrig his plan to help the Irishmen fight the Desolators.

'Batshit,' he said.

'What?'

'A trick that I used back in the day. When I fought the Romans.'

'You fought the Romans?' asked Carrig. His voice incredulous.

'Yep,' confirmed Nathaniel. 'Long story. Anyway, you collect tons of bat poo, soak it in water, filter it and then evaporate the water off. Leaves you with saltpeter. You mix that with charcoal and you have gunpowder.'

'Don't you need sulfur as well?' asked Carrig.

'Not essential. Helps it burn faster but a good blend of well-ground charcoal and saltpeter works very well. Then you use the black powder to make handheld fire grenades. The Desolators burn like dry tinder, so a few firebombs chucked in amongst them will do a world of damage.'

'Sounds good,' agreed Carrig. 'Only problem is, no bats.'

Nathaniel thought for a while. 'If I remember correctly, you can use human urine instead. Thing is, it takes a while. You need to dig a pit, line it with straw and then fill it with urine. A big pit, mind you. Then you wait six months or so, dig the whole pit up, mix with lots of water, filter it, and evaporate. Saltpeter.'

'Gross,' commented Carrig.

'True,' agreed Nathaniel. 'But not as gross as losing your mind to the Desolators.'

'True,' affirmed the Irishman.

'Also, I have another idea. I've got this guy, Roo, ex-Australian, he made a fire-fighting wagon for us. It's basically a large steel drum mounted on the back of a horse-drawn cart. The drum is attached to a bellows pump and a hose. You fill the drum with water, pump the bellows and it squirts the water at the fire. It's really effective. Can shoot water over thirty yards. Maybe more.'

'Good idea, boss,' sniggered Tad. 'If the bombs fail we can wash them to death.'

'I'm not finished, you ass,' quipped Nathaniel. 'We can fill the drums with fish oil, spray the Desolators and then, when we chuck the bombs, the whole area will become a burning, killing field.'

Carrig smiled. 'Now that would be a thing of beauty,' he said.

They discussed tactics and plans all the way back. By the time they arrived at the town, word had already gone ahead, and they were greeted as heroes. Impromptu street parties had already started, and various scratch bands of musicians were playing on street corners and in taverns. Many of the soldiers joined in but some, either too grievously wounded or simply too tired, seeked bed and rest.

The next day Nathaniel and the bulk of his men clambered back into the ice boats and returned home, leaving a small group of advisors and ambassadors to stay with Carrig.

CHAPTER 18

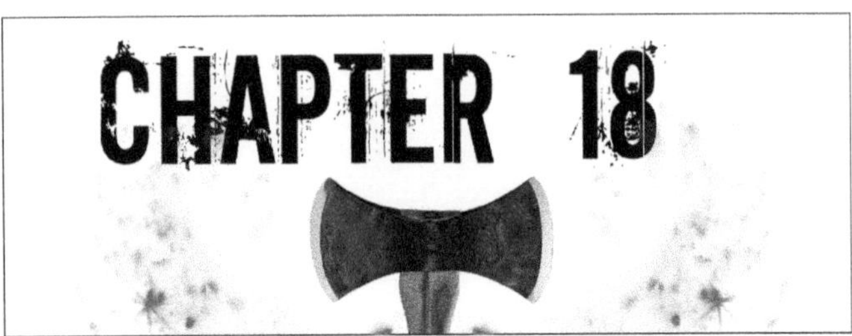

'Vandals?' asked Nathaniel.

'That's what JJ said they called themselves,' replied Roo. 'He calls them bat-people. Reckons that they look like a cross between bats and really thin people. But they refer to themselves as Vandals.'

'If my memory serves me correctly,' added Tad. 'The Vandals were a Germanic tribe, existed around the fifth century. I think that they sacked Rome at one stage. Real bad dudes.'

'Can't hold that against them,' quipped Nathaniel. 'The Romans were a proper bunch of dicks, if you ask me.'

'You're biased,' pointed out Tad.

'Didn't claim otherwise,' confirmed The Forever Man.

'Strictly speaking, they may not actually refer to themselves as Vandals,' said Gogo. 'The fact is, as far as I can work out, the magik of the pulse light is somehow allowing us to understand a human approximation of what they are saying. There is no way that they are actually speaking English or a dialect so similar that we can understand it. It's the same way that we understand the Orcs or the Fair-Folk.'

'Man,' said Tad. 'This just gets weirder and weirder. Hell, when I was with the circus we had a bearded lady, name of Dorcas, she sold popcorn, soda, that sort of thing. People thought that she was exotic. Now we've got Orcs and goblins, and bat-people and aliens.' He glanced at Roo. 'Australians.'

'Steady on,' objected Roo with a grin.

'Are they friendly?' asked Nathaniel.

Roo shrugged. 'They're not unfriendly. They haven't attacked anyone. They don't seem to have stolen any cattle or horses. Actually, they are quite timid. They tend to stay in the deep forest and keep to themselves. Mind you, we've only been aware of their existence for a week or so. Maybe they're biding their time. But I don't think so.'

'What was JJ doing on the other side of the wall?' asked the Marine

Roo shrugged. 'It's not illegal. I think that he sometimes hunts there, finds it easier. The game is more plentiful.'

'Right then,' said Nathaniel. 'I say that we put together some sort of task force to attempt contact with these Vandals. Tad, perhaps you should take a couple of men from The Ten, go the other side of the wall, track down these Vandals and see if you can communicate.'

Tad nodded.

'Next thing,' continued the Marine. 'Roo, we have a story to tell.'

And Nathaniel, with a bit of help and interjection from Tad, told Roo of the last few days. The raiders, the battles, the Desolators, and finally, his plan to combat the wraith-like enemy.

Roo listened without comment and then, as was his habit, he simply sat quietly for a while, letting his impressive brain work through the problems.

Finally, he spoke. 'Right,' he said. 'No worries. I'll set up a fire wagon. I can modify the bellows to get more pressure and put a smaller nozzle on so that it can squirt further. Maybe even sixty yards. Also, I reckon that I can fit a flint on the end of the nozzle that will ignite the oil as it leaves the hose. Turn it into a flame thrower.'

'Alright people,' said Nathaniel. 'Make it all so. I'm going to sleep for the next ten hours and woe betide anyone who wakes me. For any reason at all, I'm serious.'

Tad and Roo rose, bowed slightly, and left the room. Gogo waited for them to leave before she spoke.

'Marine,' she said. 'Milly is outside. She has been waiting for you.'

A flicker of irritation showed on Nathaniel's face before he covered it with a brittle smile.

'Be careful with her, Forever Man,' warned Gogo. 'She totters on the very edge. She loves you.'

'Yes,' answered Nathaniel. 'And I love her.'

Gogo shook her head. 'No, you don't,' she said. Her voice flat but non-accusing. A simple statement of fact. 'You feel indebted to her. You feel that you let her down. You abandoned her.'

'I did.'

'You did not. Far greater powers were at play than you, or her, realize. You left her with caring friends and as much security as you thought that she needed. The evil things that transpired had naught to do with you.'

'If I had stayed, or taken her with me, she wouldn't have been attacked. Humiliated and abused.'

'That is true. But perhaps there would now be no Free State as a result. For every action there is a corresponding result. We have been led to this point by a confluence of occurrences and any change might have ruined everything.'

'Whatever, Gogo,' said Nathaniel. 'I will not let her down again. Whatever the cost.'

'I know, my boy,' replied the old woman. 'You wouldn't be who you are if you thought in any other way. But I urge you to be careful. Show caution, think. Be stern but fair. I will show myself out and tell Milly that she can come in and see you. Give her a task of some sort. Something personal and then tell her you need to sleep. She will not bother you.'

The ancient lady bowed her farewell and left the room.

Nathaniel took a deep breath and fixed a welcoming smile on his face.

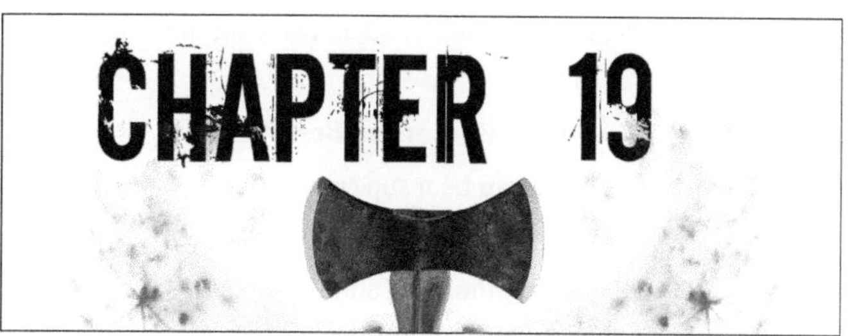

CHAPTER 19

Although it was possible to manufacture paper, even after the pulse, it was incredibly time-consuming and the end product was very rough. As a result, this meant that the easiest way to access new paper was to recycle old paper. This was done by chopping the paper up into small pieces, soaking it in lots of water and then pounding it into a pulp. This pulp was then spread thinly onto screens, dried and then pressed until it was thin enough and flat enough to be used as writing paper once again.

This was the reason that the Fair-Folk had decided, when passing their new history laws, that all existing books would not be burned but would instead be rendered down to pulp and reused.

Teams of Orcs, goblins, and worthy humans were being sent from house to house, collecting all textbooks, novels, bibles, and journals. These were loaded into horse-drawn carts and taken to central processing depots.

Hoarding books in any form was declared to be a capital crime and punishment was both swift and harsh. After the first few hangings, no one dared hide any more books.

A new class of human was introduced by the Fair-Folk, Superior humans. These superiors outranked worthies and were given extra responsibility as well as rewards. Larger houses, the right to three human servants paid for by the Fair-Folk government, first accesses to food choices and clothing and a right to trade food, horses, and cattle.

In return they governed whole areas of humanity. Collections of villages and towns were put under their administrative control and they prepared weekly and monthly reports to the Fair-folk.

A less than subtle campaign was started by the Fair-Folk using hand-painted posters depicting superior humans and carrying the slogan—

"The Best of the Best."

You too can be a superior human.

Work hard

Obey the laws and rules

Know that the Fair-Folk are here to help you

Encourage those around you to better themselves

Tell someone in charge if you see anyone breaking the rules

Be the best that you can be

Do the right thing

Be a superior human

Defacing the posters was declared a capital offense, so none were despoiled. Humans are an otherwise race but even the most rabid anti-alien considered death by hanging to be an adequate deterrent to drawing a moustache on a poster.

At the same time, lessons at schools were drastically cut and all that remained was basic math, reading and writing, and history. The history did not even bother to give a nod to reality and scholars were simply taught that mankind had driven itself to the very edge of extinction through war and barbarism, and this only stopped when the Fair-Folk took over and intervened. The Fair-Folk created law and order. They exterminated the criminal element and brought about extended peace and prosperity to all.

As soon as a child had mastered the basic 3Rs then their academic career was over, and they started training to work on the mines or on a farm.

All skilled or even semi-skilled jobs were kept for worthies, and or, superiors.

Due to the recent spate of willful sabotage, the Fair-Folk had massively expanded the number of Orc patrols. Now, thousands of groups of Orcs, in parties of five, patrolled towns, villages, main roads, and farms.

Two large areas were designated human sanctuaries and were fenced in. These areas were only accessible by humans, apart from a small contingent of Orc guards to keep the law. Humans were allowed to grow whatever they wanted and manufacture any goods, apart from weapons of war, books, paper, oil, or tools.

One of the areas was the Norfolk Broads, the other was the Romney marshes. Both areas were fine for farming sheep, but the land was not conducive for intensive farming and the weather was bitter with driving winds and little natural cover.

Technically speaking, the humans had their reserves and the Fair-Folk trumpeted their support for human freedom across the lands.

***

The Fair-Folk did not smile in the human manner. Their facial structure and muscular layout was not designed to do so. Instead, pleasure or humor or contentment was exhibited by a glottal clicking sound made in the back of the throat.

At the moment, both mage Seth Hil Nu and Commander Ammon Bat Ra were clicking.

In front of both of them lay a map. On the map were a series of wooden arrows. These markers showed the movement of troops across the land south of Hadrian's Wall. Fully six hundred thousand troops were being moved across the country, massing in the north. They were close enough to the wall to get there within two or three days hard march, but not so close as to cause alarm.

The Fair-Folk had ensured that all had been told about this military happening. It was merely a troop training exercise. Nothing more and nothing less.

And, in all fairness, Commander Ammon hoped that it would remain a mere exercise. A show of strength, necessary but not needed.

In reality, though, the troops were being massed to preempt any overt action that might occur when the next part of their plan went ahead.

And the next part of the plan was what had pleased Ammon enough to cause him to click in appreciation. Senior mage Seth Hil Nu had put together a plan using Orc Sergeant Kob and two fanatical superior humans.

The plan was simple and daring and perfect. In a day's time, during the current spring equinox tide, Sergeant Kob and his two humans were going to sneak around the wall and kidnap Milly Human. They all remembered well. She had been the one that had warned the Free State about the forthcoming Orc attack that had been repelled with such a loss of Orc and goblin life. Their intelligence also confirmed that Milly was Nathaniel Hogan's consort. Perhaps even his wife, although they weren't one hundred percent sure about that fact. Whatever the facts, they were all convinced about one major point; if they kidnapped the girl, then King Hogan would be forced to react. His ego, his place in society … his very humanity, would force him to. And that reaction could only take place in one way—he would have to launch an attack on the Fair-Folk in order to free his woman.

Ammon clicked again. These humans and their testosterone-driven thinking made them easy prey. He rubbed his hands together and moved one of the wooden arrows a little closer to the wall.

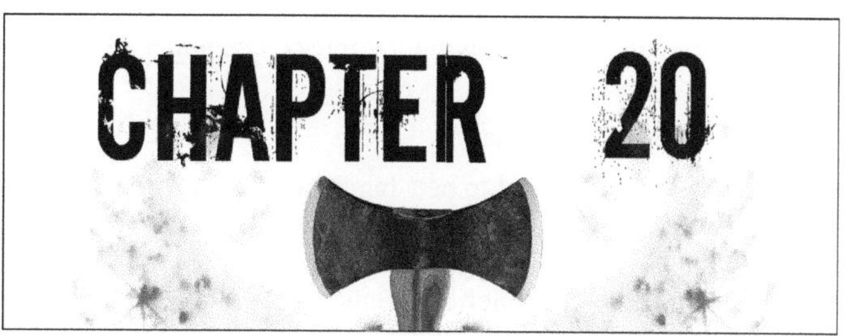

Tad went down on one knee and studied the tracks. There had been no fresh snow, so they should have been easy to follow, but they weren't. The Vandals had a habit of flying and walking in spurts. The tracks would suddenly disappear, and one would have to cast around for them, usually finding them twenty yards away, traveling in a different direction to the previous ones.

Tad had ridden to the last point where JJ had reported seeing the Vandals and had started to track them from there, leading their horses as they scanned the ground ahead of them.

With him were two other members of The Ten. Fast friends, Gareth Soames and Peter Jakes. Both men had been cast from the same mold. Six foot, muscular, taciturn. Both with a sense of humor so dry as to be almost nonexistent and a keen sense of sarcasm that was so honed that at times, even they weren't sure if they were being sarcastic or not.

Most people found them very difficult to get along with, but Tad liked and respected both of them. Plus, they were extremely good in a fight, being proficient with axe and sword.

'If they can fly, why do they walk at all?' mused Gareth.

'I suppose that it's difficult to maintain any sort of flight path in the forest,' said Tad. 'So, they walk, and when there's a gap in the trees or something, then they fly for a bit.'

Gareth nodded. 'Makes sense. How many of them do you reckon that we're following?'

Tad shook his head. 'Not entirely sure. Quite a lot. Maybe twenty. Maybe a few more. Not less though.'

The three men continued following the tracks, keeping a good look out at the same time.

'Hey,' said Peter. 'What's that?'

He pointed at what appeared to be a bundle of red and white rags piled up in a small depression in the ground. The three of them changed course and walked over to the object. As they got closer it became obvious that it wasn't a pile of rags. It was, in fact, the leftover remains of a sheep's carcass. But the animal had been torn to shreds. Blood was also scattered about the remains in a fine spray, like a myriad of tiny red jewels in the snow.

'Must be wolves,' said Gareth.

Tad shook his head. 'No ways. Men did this. Look,' he pointed at a wound that ran across the sheep's skull. It had been split in twain with a blow from a sharp blade. 'Sword strike,' continued the little big man. 'Also, here, and here.' He showed where the legs had been sliced off.

'What about this?' asked Gareth, as he looked at a gaping hole that had been torn in the sheep's stomach. It was obvious that something with large jaws had torn open the abdominal cavity and pulled the internal organs out.

'Maybe wolves stripped the body after the men had killed it,' ventured Peter.

Tad shook his head. 'No wolf tracks.'

The three of them scouted the ground, lifting leaves and checking out broken twigs and other signs.

'No human tracks either,' said Gareth. 'This doesn't make any sense.'

Tad pointed at a series of marks in the snow. 'What are those?'

They all peered closely at the series of crisscrossed lines that were spread out around the body.

Gareth shrugged. 'No track that I've ever seen. Looks like someone made patterns with a handful of sticks. Very strange.'

'Well, come on,' said Tad. 'Let's keep to the task at hand. The Vandal's tracks lead that way.' He stood up from his kneeling position and set off after the Vandals. Gareth and Peter followed.

'This is fun,' quipped Gareth.

'Immense,' agreed Peter. 'In fact, I haven't had so much fun since I last tracked down a group of unknown, potentially vicious, flying alien creatures.'

'With any luck they'll breath fire as well,' enthused Gareth.

'Just peachy,' added Peter.

'Shut it, guys,' ordered Tad. 'You're not half as humorous as you seem to think.'

'Cruel, master,' stage-whispered Gareth. 'Not appreciate Peter and Gareth's keen sense of wit.'

Tad shook his head in mock weariness and they plodded on.

The going was slow with lots of stopping and checking and retracing their steps. They stopped next to a stream at lunchtime, eating some dried meat, hunks of cheese and apples. They fed the horses some oats

and encouraged them to drink their full from the icy stream.

Tad stamped his feet and rubbed his hands together in an attempt to warm up and they started on their way again. They followed the intermittent tracks through a thick copse of trees and over a small knoll. As they broached the knoll they were greeted with a sight that froze them to the spot in horror.

The entire area was covered in blood and flesh and fur. Tattered shreds of meat hung from the lowered boughs of some of the trees. Jagged ends of broken bones poked out from the snow and pools of frozen blood lay in puddles of death across the clearing.

Pete and Gareth drew their swords at the same time and, like magik, a pair of knives appeared in Tad's hands, ready to throw.

With Tad at the front, the three formed a V and walked slowly forward, picking their steps carefully to avoid the blood and gore. It took less than a minute to ascertain that the ragged remains scattered about the clearing were not human; nevertheless, the sight was still very disturbing.

Tad picked up a piece of bloodstained fur. 'Wolf.'

Gareth nodded his agreement. 'Looks like a whole pack. Ten, twelve. All dead.'

'The same sword cuts,' said Tad as he knelt and studied the remains. 'Also, more of these strange stick patterns. Once again, no human tracks and no Vandal tracks. Guys,' he continued. 'I reckon that we've got a third party here. Some sort of creature that we haven't seen before. And I'll tell you something for nothing—whatever it is … it's bad. From what I can garner from the limited amount of tracks, I guess that there was no more than three of them. Against a pack of full grown wolves. And I can't see any evidence of injury done to them. I don't know about you but anything that can take on this many wolves with impunity and leave them torn to shreds like this … well … whatever they are, they scare the crap out of me.'

'This isn't right,' agreed Gareth. 'This wasn't self-defense, it was simply butchery. Killing for killings sake.' He spat on the ground in disgust as he sheathed his broadsword. 'It's unnecessary.'

'Let's forge on,' said Tad as he grabbed his horse's reins and led it from the bloodied clearing, eyes darting from side to side as they warily searched the surrounding shadows.

After another hour of trudging through the snow Tad raised his hand, fist clenched in the traditional stop warning. 'We're being watched,' he said, his voice only a little above a whisper.

'Where?' asked Gareth.

'Not sure,' answered the little big man. 'Can't actually see anyone. But I can feel it. They're close. Real close.'

All three scanned the surrounds, eyes slatted in concentration.

And then suddenly and without warning a creature appeared in front of them, seeming to simply pop into existence out of thin air.

Tad let out a grunt of surprise. Peter and Gareth went for their swords, but Tad held his hand up.

'Wait,' he said. 'Don't draw your weapons. Remember, we're here in peace. Fact finding not fighting.'

Tad stared at the creature; it stood about five foot tall, much the same height as the little big man, a triangular face, big eyes, a scrawny body with thin arms and legs. And a pair of large leathern wings draped down from its shoulders like a long brown cloak. Judging by JJ's descriptions this was definitely a Vandal.

Tad took a step forward, his hands held out in front of him, palms up to show that he had no weapons. But the creature hissed in fear, shrank back and promptly disappeared.

'He's gone,' exclaimed Peter.

Tad squinted at the place where the Vandal had just been. He tilted his head slightly and then he saw it. 'No,' he denied. 'He's still there. Look closely. Sort of use the corner of your eye.'

Both Gareth and Peter did as the little big man had advised.

'Well, I'll be,' whispered Peter. 'I think that I can see him. How the hell is he doing that?'

As soon as you knew that the Vandal had, in fact, not disappeared it was possible to see, not so much him, but the evidence of him. The air around it wavered slightly. Like a heat wave, or mirage. If you squinted just right, you could see a vague shimmering shape that outlined the creature.

As the Vandal realized that he was no longer invisible he flashed back into focus.

Tad clapped his hands in delight. 'Damn, that's clever,' he said.

The Vandal looked surprised at Tad's reaction and then it preened itself, shivering its wings and standing tall, a look of pride on its small, weasel-like face.

Tad approached again, both hands held out, palms up. The Vandal stared at him, cocked its head to one side and imitated Tad, holding its claw-like hands out.

'Greetings,' said Tad.

The Vandal shrieked and then chattered back with a series of clicks and pops interspersed with more shrieks. 'Damn,' said Tad. 'I thought that JJ said that we could understand them.'

The Vandal stopped babbling, stared at Tad, and then spoke.

'Gree-tings, hu-man.'

'We have come in peace,' continued Tad.

'Take us to your leader,' quipped Gareth sarcastically.

The Vandal looked at Gareth. 'Lea-der,' it repeated.

'Shut up, Gareth,' snapped Tad. 'This is serious.'

'Ga-reth,' said the Vandal. 'Shut-up.'

Both Peter and Gareth burst out laughing. The Vandal made a strange chirruping noise, like a tin full of crickets. Tad rightly assumed that this was his version of laughter.

'Come, hu-mans,' said the Vandal. 'Fo-llow me to lea-der.'

The creature scuttled off, turning its head every now and then to check that it was being followed. The three warriors trotted behind it.

Every now and then the Vandal would stretch its wings open and flutter forward, taking off and landing ten yards forward. This strange combination of flying and walking moved it along at a pace and the three humans and their horses had to shift to keep up.

After ten minutes the Vandal took a sharp right into a thickly wooded part of the forest, ducking below hanging boughs. The smell of wood smoke and roasting meats assailed Tad's nostrils and set his mouth watering. He was still hungry after their less than satisfying trail lunch.

They entered a clearing in the trees. Rude shelters had been constructed from branches and leaves and a row of open fires lay across the center of the clearing. Braces of various birds and rabbits had been spitted over the fires and over twenty Vandals were squatting around the fires, their wings curled about themselves for warmth.

As the three humans entered the clearing some of the creatures went invisible. Some stayed where they were for all to see and one stood up to greet them.

He stood slightly taller than the rest and when he unfurled his wings it was apparent that he had a much larger wingspan.

The first Vandal that they met pointed at the larger creature.

'Lea-der,' it said.

Tad stepped forward and bowed. Peter and Gareth followed suit.

The leader pointed at himself. 'Char-rek, lea-der. Chief.' Then he pointed at the other Vandal that they had met. 'Grim-son. Not lea-der. Scout.'

Tad touched his own chest. 'Tad. Warrior-chief of The Ten. He pointed to each of his friends in turn. Gareth of The Ten, not chief. Peter of The Ten, not chief.'

'Well met,' said Char-rek. 'Please, eat with us.' He showed them to a spot next to the fire and clapped his hands. More Vandals appeared from the shelters. They looked the same as the other Vandals. Naked but for a brief breechclout. Except for the fact that the new Vandals were obviously female.

They lay rough wooden serving platters next to the men and served out the roasted game, fruit, and raw vegetables together with wooden bowls of a milky liquid.

Char-rek started to eat and gestured for the humans to do the same. The meat was delicious, lightly spiced and cooked perfectly. Tad picked up a bowl of the milky liquid and sniffed it. His nostrils tingled slightly from the smell. Astringent, vaguely spicy. He took a sip. The raw alcohol evaporated inside his mouth and went straight into his nasal cavities making him throw his head back and sneeze. All about him the Vandals erupted with the strange cricket-like sound that showed that they were laughing.

Tad smiled embarrassedly and took another sip, ready for the shock this time. The drink burned like fire but wasn't altogether unpleasant, leaving an aftertaste of cinnamon and cloves.

'What is it?' he asked Grim-son.

'Is drink.'

'I know that,' countered Tad. 'What is it made from?'

'Sap,' said Grim-son. 'Sap from that tree.' He pointed at a birch. 'We fer-ment and dis-till.'

Both Peter and Gareth tried the drink and nodded appreciatively. Grim-son looked pleased that they enjoyed it.

While they ate, Tad used the time to study the creatures more closely. They were obviously fairly primitive. They appeared to be nomadic and had little in the way of clothing or ornaments. Their weapons, such as they were, consisted of short swords of bronze; daggers of either bronze or flint and light wooden spears with flint tips. He could see no evidence of steel nor ranged weapons such as bows or slings.

'Do you not possess steel weapons?' asked the little big man.

Grim-son shook his head. 'The gray metal hurts us.'

'How?'

'Please pass small knife,' asked Grim-son.

Tad drew a small throwing dagger from his sleeve and passed it handle first to the Vandal.

Grim-son took it with a look of distaste on his face. Then, carefully, he held the blade close to his skin. Light shimmered about the naked steel and Grim-son's skin puckered up beneath it. He drew the blade away and a raised red weal stood out on his arm where the metal had been.

'It hurts,' he said. 'Also. No can dis-appear. Gray metal hold the light so we cannot bend it.' He handed the dagger back.

Tad nodded. 'I see.' He turned to Gareth and Peter. 'Their cloaking skills are effected by steel. They must be based on some sort of magnetism. Using a magnetic field to bend the light around them so that they appear invisible. The iron in steel would prevent that. Interesting.'

'Yeah,' said Peter. 'Or not. Ask them about the wolves that we saw all chopped up. Was that them?'

'You ask them,' countered Tad.

'Oh, I wouldn't dare,' continued Peter. 'What with being a "not-chief" and merely a simple warrior. I'd rather leave all of the wordy stuff to the chiefs, if you don't mind.' He tugged at his forelock to reinforce his argument and added a 'Kind sir,' on the end of the sentence to rub it in further.

'Stop being such an ass,' smiled Tad.

'Pe-ter,' said Grim-son. 'Ass.'

Once again, the air was filled with the high-pitched chittering of Vandal laughter.

Peter laughed. 'We saw some wolves on the way here,' he addressed chief Char-rek.

'What is wol-ves?' asked the chief.

Peter thought for a few seconds before he answered. 'He held his hand out in front of him to show the approximate height. 'About this high. This long. Furry, big teeth. Like a dog. A hunter. Carnivore. Travels in packs'

Char-rek nodded. 'Beasts that eat and hunt together, hunter-eaters. Yes, we know them.'

'Well, we came across a pack of them. Big pack. But they were all dead. They'd been chopped up something horrible. Pieces everywhere. I was wondering, was that anything to do with you guys?'

Both Char-rek and Grim-son reacted immediately, breaking out into loud hoots and shrieks, bouncing up and down as they did so. The rest of the tribe joined in, screaming and hollering, their squeals so high-pitched as to cause the humans actual pain.

Eventually they calmed down to a level that Tad could pose a question.

'Hey, what the hell is going on?'

Chief Char-rek stared at the little big man, his face a mask of desolation.

'It is the En-emy,' he said. 'Only the En-emy could kill a pack of hunter-eaters so easily and with such violence. We thought that we had es-caped from, them,' continued the chief. 'A-cross the great divide we came, hi-ding and run-ning. Al-ways staying in sha-dow. But they have found us. They are here.'

'Who are the Enemy?' asked Tad

The Vandal turned to face the little big man and he took a deep shuddering breath before he answered.

'We call them the Annihilators. They are death,' he said. 'Death to all. To you, to me … all.'

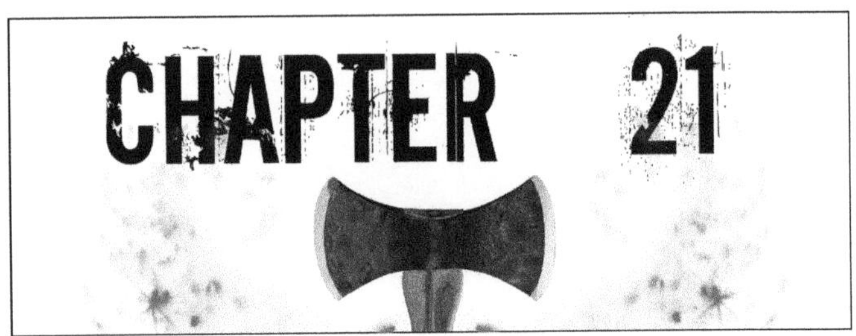

The three humans had stayed the night with the Vandals, but after they had found out that the Enemy had arrived the creatures had become uncommunicative. Sullen and tense.

Tad had risen before the sun and kicked Peter and Gareth awake. They needed to set off with some margin of speed as there was a lot that Nathaniel needed to know.

The little big man had invited the group of Vandals to accompany them so that they could come to the Free State and meet with The Forever Man. But Char-rek had refused, saying that they would stay in the deep forest. Hiding.

Tad tried to get more information about the Enemy but Char-rek would not clarify nor expand on anything. He merely warned Tad that the Enemy was plentiful and very dangerous.

Prepare for war, he had told Tad. And when it comes, we will help. I will gather all of my people, he had said, and we will find you.

They had just had an unappetizing trail lunch when they came across a pile of mutilated cows. The wounds were consistent with what they had seen before. Massive sword strikes and savage tearing bites. Some flesh had been consumed, but once again, it seemed that the primary reason for the killings was simple butchery.

The three humans rode past the bloody site and continued on the trail, eyes peeled for any would-be attackers or sightings of anything out of the ordinary.

Eventually, the forest started to thin out slightly and the trail became easier to follow, straighter and wider. As they turned a gentle curve, a cottage came into sight. A trickle of smoke rose from the chimney as well as from two large piles of hay and mud on the right-hand side of the abode.

'Charcoal burning,' said Tad, pointing at the two smoldering heaps. 'They get cords of wood, stack them up, light them and then cover the whole thing with damp hay and mud. Lets the wood burn very slowly and makes charcoal.'

As they rode closer they could see that the door was hanging open, canting crookedly off its hinges like a drunken sailor propped against a bar. The top corner looked as though it had been sheared off with an axe or massive sword.

Both Peter and Gareth drew their blades and Tad flicked a throwing knife from his arm sheath into his right hand. They walked their horses up close to the cottage and dismounted.

Tad took point and pushed the broken door fully open, keeping to the one side so as not to outline himself in the doorway.

'Hello,' he called out. 'Is there anybody there?'

He could hear the faint crackle of the fire burning in the hearth, the wood popping and hissing as the flames consumed it. But no other sound was apparent.

The little big man stepped inside and surveyed the room.

It was a complete charnel house. Vaguely recognizable pieces of human were scattered about the room as if someone had torn the charcoal maker apart in a fit of childish pique and thrown his body parts all about the room.

The now familiar hack wounds were prevalent as were the ravening tooth marks. It was obvious that this poor charcoal burner had fallen victim to the Enemy. The Annihilators.

Without talking, the three men collected all of the parts that they could and wrapped them in a sheet. Then they dug a grave, choosing a spot near to the smoldering charcoal heaps because the ground had been thawed out from the heat and made digging possible.

Afterwards, they checked the stables and the paddocks but found no sign of horses or livestock, dead or alive. The animals had obviously escaped into the surrounding forest during the attack.

'Come on, guys,' urged Tad. 'We need to get moving. Nathaniel needs to know about these Annihilator dudes, looks like it's going to be a problem that we need to address. If we push through, we could make the wall by nightfall.'

They mounted up and proceeded on their way. They rode in silence, still stunned at the level of violence that they had seen, eyes and ears straining to catch any false moves in the shadows or the undergrowth. Hand close to weapons as they rode.

Slowly the track became a road that broadened to become a major artery. The remains of one of the pre-pulse highways that led to the north.

Tad heard them first, his hearing being the sharpest of the three.

'Something's coming,' he said. 'Lots of somethings. Move.'

The three of them dismounted and led their horses off the road and deep into the forest. Gareth cut a branch off a tree and went back to the road to brush over any sign of their tracks.

The warriors tethered their horses in a copse of trees, well protected from line of sight of the road and then they dropped and crawled forward to see what was coming.

The three did not have to wait for long.

The Orcs marched into view, ten abreast across the road, the earth shuddering in time to their marching feet.

The horde drew level with the humans and marched past in a never-ending column. All three watched in disbelief as the minutes crept by.

Hundreds marched past, then thousands. And slowly, as the hours passed, the count went into the tens of thousands. Orcs, goblins, trolls, mounted human worthies and even a few Fair-Folk being carried in their customary litters.

The sun was low on the horizon when the last of the Orcs tramped past, leaving the road a morass of mud and ice and splintered pieces of old tarmacadam.

'Well that's not something that you see every day,' said Tad. 'How many do you reckon?' he asked Peter.

'Not sure. Umm … all of them?'

Gareth laughed. 'We wish. I think around eighty thousand.'

Tad nodded. 'Yep. I figured a hundred thousand. Let's get to the horses. We cut through the woods and circle ahead of them. Nathaniel needs to know about this as soon as.'

They ran to the horses, mounted, and set off at a fast trot.

Tad shook his head in disbelief as they rode. 'I tell you something, boys,' he addressed his two friends. 'We're gonna need a set of stepladders soon. What with Vandals and Orc armies and psychotic Annihilators, it won't be long until the level of crap that's raining down on us gets above head level and we drown in the stuff.'

Peter and Gareth laughed. But it was a sound without humor. Rough and forced. A mere acknowledgement of their predicament as opposed to a voicing of hilarity.

***

Nathaniel scrubbed his eyes with the heels of his hands in an attempt to grind some moisture into them. Tad and his two friends had arrived late that evening, just before the Marine was about to retire for the night, and they had delivered their news.

Nathaniel had then sent someone to fetch Roo and general Carson and he had made Tad repeat the whole thing.

Now the group of six men sat in contemplative silence, waiting for Nathaniel to say something.

'There have been reports of more Orc armies,' he said to Tad. Over the last three days another five columns of over one hundred thousand each have approached the vicinity of the wall. A total of six hundred thousand warriors stretching from Carlisle to Tynemouth.' He leaned forward and poured himself some water from a jug on the table. 'The Vandals,' he said to Tad. 'Friend or foe?'

'Definite friends,' affirmed Tad. 'Not sure what good they can do militarily wise, not even sure how many of them that there are, but friends, nevertheless.'

Nathaniel nodded. 'Good. Friends are good. We appear to have gone long on enemies, so we'll take whatever allies we can find. Now, these Annihilators. What gives?'

Tad shrugged. 'Bad. Again, not sure how many of them there are but I can assure you, even a few will be a problem. The Vandals are well scared of them. Not much else that I can say.'

'Right,' said the Marine. 'For the moment we can leave them out of the equation. I think that it's pretty obvious that the Fair-Folk are making a move. You don't simply move six hundred thousand troops into an area without some sort of plan. I reckon that an attack is imminent. General, your thoughts.'

Carson nodded in agreement. 'I think that we need to stand to. Call up everyone and man the wall with all that we have. Reserves, militia. Everyone.'

'I concur,' said Nathaniel. 'Roo, what's the food and supply situation? How many people do we need to leave free for food production, crop maintenance, etcetera?'

'We can use the women and children for that. Call up every able-bodied man over fourteen. Also, I suggest that we speak to Gogo as soon as possible and get some teams of her young magicians out along the wall to provide shields. Also,' continued Roo. 'I sent one of those converted water cannons to your Irish mates. You remember? The ones that I turned into flame throwers.'

'Good,' said Nathaniel. 'How did it work?'

'Awesome.' Grinned Roo. 'In fact, I've got the lads making another ten to distribute along the wall. They're weapons of note and I reckon that they will come in real handy pretty soon.'

The six of them talked way into the night, organizing the details of the army's full mobilization. Distribution of spare weapons, arrows, horses and hay, bandages, food, water, and more. The minutia of details that wars are won or lost by. Latrines, cookhouses, and sleeping quarters. Dull, without glory but ultimately almost as important as the actual battle plan itself.

Finally, as the gray of false dawn crept into the open window, Nathaniel called it a night, and all went their separate ways to catch a few hours of exhausted sleep.

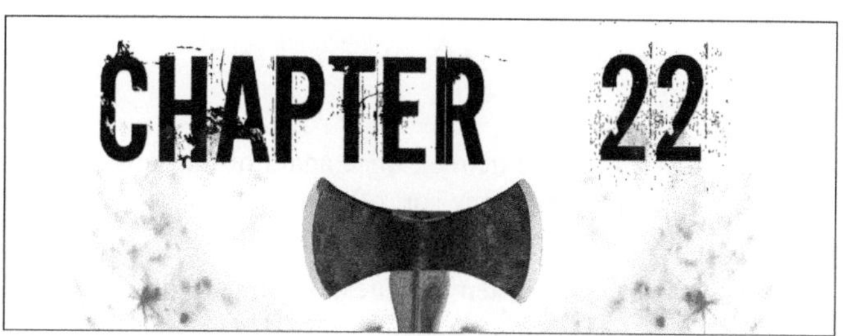

A circular, or lenticular, cloud appeared in the sky above the Castlerigg Stone circle in Cumbria, rising high into the atmosphere like a gigantic UFO. Its edges flickered with the bright colors of irisation, turning the normal pale white of the cloud into an extravagance of iridescent mother-of-pearl. A swirling mass of purple and scarlet and red.

Blue-white light arced from stone to stone and the air was filled with the smell of ozone and steel, as immeasurable powers were unleashed. Powers that were so large as to be impossible to create without the massive amounts of gamma-radiation that had drenched the earth's atmosphere after the pulse.

Power in quantities so large as to enable a rift in time and space to be torn between the here and the now. Slowly the arcing lights centered on each other, cackling and fizzing as they joined into a circle about the stones. And, in the center of that circle—a black hole.

A single creature stepped through, strode into the heather and stood, head swiveling back and forth as it surveyed the land. The mist swirled about, coating its armor with a delicately jeweled sheen that brought out the vibrant colors that seemed to have been lacquered onto its surface. Predominantly green and yellow with vivid stripes of red and blue interspersed with black borders.

The creature stood eight foot tall, a foreshortened torso and long legs that bent backwards at the knee. Its feet were like bundles of sticks tied together with short sharp claws on the end. Two sets of arms sprouted from its torso. The lower set ended in claw-like hands. Three fingers and a long thumb complete with long claws. The upper set ended in what appeared to be a two-foot long blade made from the same material as its armor and lacquered in the same gaudy colors.

On its head was a full-face helmet, once again of the same material and colors. It had a hinged jaw and some sort of reinforced glass or Plexiglas eye coverings that stood out, bug-like from the front.

It stood alone for almost ten minutes, sniffing the air, and quietly observing.

Then it threw back its head and shrieked.

Instantly, hundreds of other like creatures poured forth from the black hole in the circle of arced lights. They ran in a jerky, stop-motion manner, their armor clicking noisily as they did so. Like massive, deadly wind-up toys.

With robotic precision they formed into ranks and then stood still, only their heads swiveling from side to side as they surveyed the surrounds.

The circle of arc-light stuttered and flared and then another batch of creatures swarmed out. These were ostensibly the same as the foot soldiers, but they were smaller and had wings.

They buzzed back and forth across the sky, looking. Searching. Then they split up into five different groups and flew off in different directions.

Half an hour later they all returned, conferred, formed up into an arrow formation and flew off together. The foot soldiers followed them at pace, clicking and bouncing along as they did so.

They were heading directly towards the village of Keswick some three miles away.

Before the pulse Keswick had been a large town but now it was a small farming village of some nine hundred unsuspecting souls, confident of the fact that they were ensconced safely, deep inside the Free State.

Protected by The Forever Man and his army.

Safe.

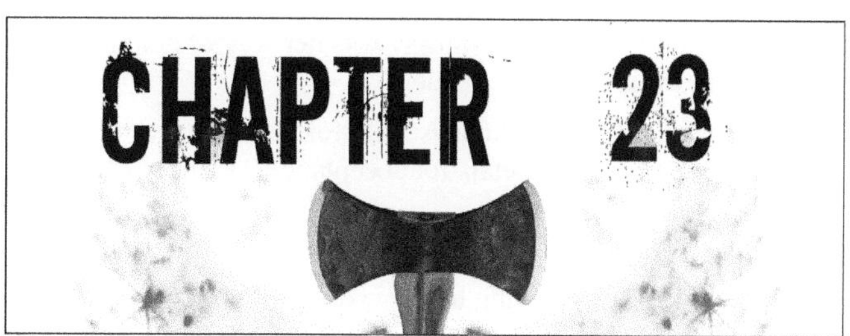

CHAPTER 23

Milly took a bite of her apple as she walked, chewing slowly and deliberately. Counting as she did so. Thirty times. It was something that her mother had once told her. Chew each mouthful thirty times.

It was the only thing that she remembered about her mother. She couldn't remember the color of her hair, or her eyes. Not her smell or even the timbre of her voice. She couldn't remember her dying in front of her.

All that she did remember from that day was Nathaniel. Appearing like a god and killing the bad men and taking her away. Protecting her. Caring for her.

Chew each mouthful thirty times a day.

The sum total of her childhood memories before she met The Forever Man.

Nathaniel had returned from chasing the raiders, or whatever excuse he had dreamed up, and was, even now, resting at his abode. So, she had decided that she would use this time to create a tussy-mussy. It was an old-fashioned idea that she had seen Gogo and her walking folk practice. Basically, a bunch of flowers. However, the end product was much more than that. It was created and tied together in a specific way and contained particular herbs and flowers that were combined together in a precise order to achieve a desired effect.

In this case, she wanted to open Nathaniel's mind to the idea of loving her. She had discussed things with Gogo and the old lady had told her that you simply could not make someone love you. And Milly had whole heartedly agreed. Gogo had looked pleased, as if the two of them were agreeing on something. But Milly knew that Nathaniel already loved her. Just as she loved him. It was merely the fact that he was too noble. Too self-sacrificing to admit it and the tussy-mussy was her way of helping to prize open the oyster to reveal the pearl inside.

She needed myrtle for love, honeysuckle for devotion, ivy to represent marriage or wedded love, rose petals for acceptance, lavender for devotion, and finally basil, for sexual love.

Ivy, myrtle, and basil wouldn't be a problem, roses and lavender were a maybe. But honeysuckle was going to prove difficult to find.

She had wandered quite far from the village by the wall, heading for an area that she knew lavender flowered in during the hotter months, when she heard a noise in the trees. A scuttling sound, like a large animal. A deer or perhaps a badger.

She stopped and listened, but all was quiet once again, so she continued walking, her mind on the flowers that she was searching for.

The first inkling that she had of danger was when she was actually grabbed from behind. Two strong arms were thrown roughly around her, and a weight bore her to the ground.

'Got you, my lovely,' rasped a voice in her ear. 'Now, don't scream or struggle and we won't hurt you. Right?'

Milly said nothing, and the man stood up and pulled her to her feet. There were two of them. Clad in dark, rough woven clothing, carrying short swords and leather knapsacks that obviously contained food and water. Both were unwashed and unshaven, and Milly could smell the stink of their bodies and their breath as they stood close to her.

One pulled out a length of rope from his pocket. 'Now, girley,' he said. 'We're going to tie your arms behind your back but leaving your legs free so that you can walk. If you make a noise or drag your heels then we will hurt you. Do you understand?'

Milly nodded, her face expressionless.

He stepped forward, holding the rope out in front of him. 'Turn around,' he commanded.

Milly started to turn, but as she did so, she pulled a short, concealed dagger from inside her blouse, and turning, she whipped her arm around and plunged the blade into the man's right eye. He howled in pain and dropped the rope.

Milly pulled the knife free and swung again, slicing it through his throat, severing his windpipe and carotid arteries. He sank to the ground, grasping at his ruined throat in a vain attempt to stop his life's blood pumping out of the deep slash in his neck.

The other man drew his short sword, but Milly was too quick for him. She leapt forward and jabbed at him, the blade of her razor-sharp knife hitting him in the cheek and slicing his face open to the bone. Then she spun again and slammed the blade deep into the side of his neck, working it back and forth as she did so.

Without waiting to see what effect her last blow had achieved, she turned and ran as fast as she could, her breath burning in her lungs and her limbs shaking from reaction.

She blundered through bushes and low hanging branches, heedless of the cuts to her face and legs as she ran. Her desperate need to escape driving her beyond normal limits of speed and exhaustion.

Finally, she came across a well-used hunter's trail and she slowed down to get her bearings. She held her breath and willed her heart to stop slamming against her chest as she listened carefully for any noise of pursuit.

There was none.

Sitting down on a fallen tree bough she put her head between her knees for a while, drawing deep breaths and waiting for the blood to stop thundering in her head. Eventually she felt almost normal again.

Then she pulled her hair back into a ponytail, stood up and walked straight into the waiting arms of Orc Sergeant Kob. Before she could scream he cuffed her with an open hand on her temple, rendering her unconscious.

Then he took a letter from his pack, forced it into a cleft at the top of a three foot high stick, pegged the stick into the ground in the middle of the track, picked Milly up and started to run, his mission accomplished.

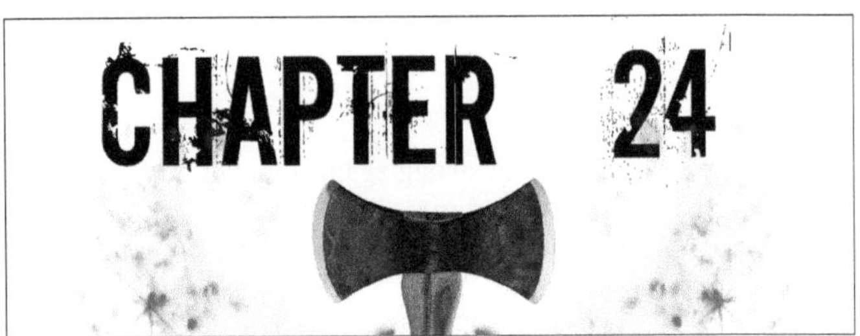

The horses swept down from the west. Fully two hundred and fifty-five thousand of them galloping at full tilt. An army the size of which had never been seen before in recorded human history.

The Xai army facing the horsemen had left the cover of the city walls and were arrayed, two hundred thousand strong, in block ranks of ten thousand. They stretched in an unbroken wall of shields ten miles wide and ten men deep.

The horde of Mongol horsemen charging down on them covered an area of ten miles wide by ten miles deep.

As each individual mounted warrior got within bow range, they released their arrows and wheeled away in order to give the next wave of mounted archers room to do the same. Their timing and discipline was impeccable. Storms of arrows fell from the sky in a continual avalanche of wood and steel.

By the time the first of the arrows struck the massed troops there were another three waves already in the air. At any one stage there were over one hundred and fifty thousand iron-tipped messengers of death plunging towards the ranks of the Xai army, with a combined weight of over half of a ton.

The arrow storm simply decimated the Xai's, driving them to their knees, punching through their armor, and killing them in their thousands.

Then the horde split and wheeled left and right, opening the way for the fifty thousand heavy cavalry with their lancers and curved sabers.

The plains ran red with blood and Genghis Khan raised his sword above his head in victory and shouted to all, 'I am a god.'.

You were/will be there ...

The Hittite king, Mutawalli and his allies, had arrayed their troops along the foothills of the mountain range of Kadesh on the border of the Hittite empire. Fully twenty thousand men, heavily armored with great shields of bronze. The king was confident that he would best the Egyptian Ramsess II and his tiny force of a mere six thousand.

And then the earth trembled as a noise arose from the desert. A noise akin to thunder. And with it the snorting and champing of thousands upon thousands of horses.

When Mutawalli stared out across the desert he could see naught but a massive cloud of dust coming towards him and he shivered in superstitious awe. Because he knew that the gods of the Egyptians were many and powerful.

But, as the dust storm got closer, he saw that it was, in fact, being produced by an army of chariots. Clad in silver and bronze and gold they were. Each carrying a rider and an archer. Drawn by two or three or even four horses. Razor-sharp blades protruded from the boss of their wheels, fluting as they sliced the air, spinning in silver blurs of death.

And then they struck the Hittite shield wall and tore through it as if it were mere papyrus sheeting. Rending and grinding and killing.

And Ramasess II raised his hands above his head and gave thanks to his gods.

You were/will be there ...

Colonel Paul Tibbets had named the Boeing-B29 Superfortress Bomber after his mother, *Enola Gay*.

After approximately six hours of flight time the aircraft and crew were, as planned, flying at 31060 feet altitude. The bomb bay doors were opened, and the package was released at exactly 8:15 Hiroshima time.

Little Boy took forty-three seconds to fall to its predetermined detonation height of 1968 feet.

In the resultant explosion over five square miles of the city was destroyed and over one hundred thousand people died.

Colonel Tibbets buried his head in his hands and prayed to his God for forgiveness.

You were/will be there ...

The series VII interstellar warship, Solar Enterprise, of the Earth's first fleet rang battle stations the moment that it came out of light speed. All weapons were brought to bear on the class three planet, ninth from the sun in the Judabar system.

Eriteam was a small blue-green planet with a population of six billion and it was a member of the Equal Life alliance, a loose affiliation of twenty-two planets that had, some two weeks prior, declared war on the Earth hegemony.

Earth's leadership had decided that an example would be made. They simply could not afford a long protracted war at this moment.

Admiral Simeon N'Dlovu and ship's Captain Peta Petrokov stood two yards apart. Each held a key in their right hands.

'On my mark,' said the admiral. 'Three, two, mark.'

Both keys were inserted. The screen above them lit up.

'Again,' continued the admiral. 'Three, two, mark.' Both keys turned one revolution clockwise.

The screen counted down from ten to zero. On zero the ships fission cannon pulsed twice. The planet of Eriteam ceased to exist.

For men had now become as powerful as the gods.

You were/will be there ...

The tall insect-like warriors stormed into the peaceful village, shrieking their war cries, the new risen sun reflecting off their garishly lacquered armor.

Above them, smaller winged versions of the same, dove and tumbled through the air, dropping boulders onto roofs, and smashing chimneystacks to the ground.

Surprised villagers ran from their cottages, armed with whatever weapons that they had to hand. Swords, axes, pitchforks, and wooden cudgels. But their resistance was utterly futile. The enemy attacked as if they were all berserkers, screeching and shrieking. Their lower set of arms they used for grasping their opponents while the upper set of bladed appendages hacked and chopped at them. Slashing, dismembering, and beheading.

And the Unicorn spoke again—*They are here ...*

The Forever Man jerked awake, his head throbbed with both pain and memories.

Memories that were so intense and real that he could still smell the air, the earth, and sand. The people.

The banging continued, and it took him a few moments to realize that someone was actually hammering on the door.

He stumbled out of bed and went to the front door. Tad pushed past him into the room, behind him was Roo and Gareth of The Ten.

Tad thrust a folded piece of paper into Nathaniel's hands.

'Read this, it's a demand from the Fair-Folk. Gareth found it on the lower game trail. He also found a couple of dead bodies close by. Milly has been kidnapped.' He continued, 'The Fair-Folk have her and they want you to present yourself to them in return for her safety.'

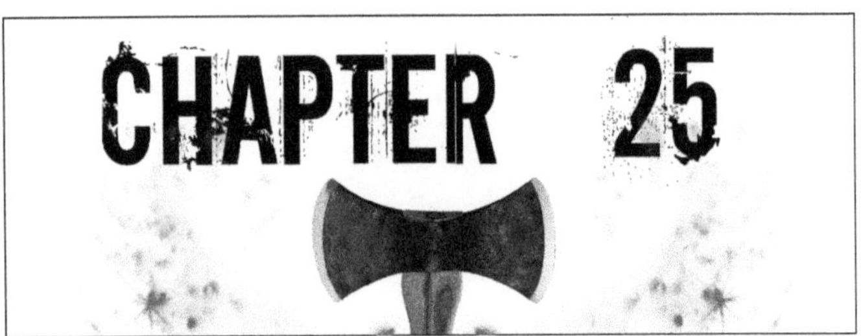

Father Donald Haven had been a priest for over forty years. He had found his calling in his early twenties and, after his year of discernment, he had been recommended for training. The next six years had been spent at theological college from which he qualified with a PhD in theological philosophy.

He had gone on to work in Africa, South America, and India before coming home and requesting a small diocese in Wiltshire. The church had complied, and he had lived many happy years there. He had never married, always being of the feeling that the Lord was more than enough companionship for him, and his flock were his children and his family and his friends.

After the pulse, he had done all that he could to help those around him, and luckily, the area where he lived had been relatively free of the roaming bands of thugs and criminals that had become so prevalent after the world had been driven backwards into the Dark Ages.

When the Fair-Folk had first arrived, Father Haven had suffered a brief crisis of faith, but after much prayer and contemplation, he had come to the conclusion that the Fair-Folk and their minions must also be part of the Lord's great plan, and as such, should also be treated as God's children.

At first, they had shown themselves to be as fair as their name. They had crushed the rogue element and brought law and order back to the land. They had encouraged production and trade and they had started a system of couriers and message delivery that stretched across the length and breadth of the land.

Over time their rules had become harsher and harsher. More draconian as opposed to merciful and sympathetic.

And then they had outlawed the owning of bibles. It was then that father Haven had realized that, as opposed to being God's children they were, instead, the spawn of Satan and he had done all that he could to subtly preach against them.

It had proven difficult. Church congregations had fallen to almost nil as people blamed God for the pulse, the Fair-Folk, the hardships, and disease. Still, the father tried his hardest. Even now, he sat at his rickety old desk in his cottage, a single candle burning for light, as he handwrote a bible. It was not perfect, and almost every page was on a different size and texture of paper ranging from laid woven to newsprint to recycled brown wrapping.

But paper was incredibly hard to come by, with the Fair-Folk ban on any individual below superior human owning any. Also, the father was writing from memory. However, it would suffice, and once he had one, then he would save and beg enough paper for a second and a third. It would take him many years, but the Lord's word would live on.

Using a piece of stone, he rubbed a sharp point into the stick of charcoal that he was writing with and continued. Slow, careful strokes. The word eternal, written illegally by candlelight in the hand of an old man who hoped that his memory was serving him correctly.

The door to the cottage literally exploded into the room, such was the force with which it was kicked in. Two Orcs, a goblin, and a human rushed into the room.

The human pointed at the priest. 'There,' he shouted. 'I told you.'

The Orcs grabbed Father Haven under his shoulders, lifting him up from his chair. The goblin scuttled over, grabbed one of the pieces of paper off the desk and quickly perused it. Then he started to load all of the papers into a sack, both the blank ones and the written.

'Well done,' grunted the goblin as he addressed the human. 'You should get a promotion to worthy for this. You can be proud of yourself.'

Father Haven looked at the young man that he had known since his birth. A man that he had christened and baptized.

'Jonathan,' he asked. 'Why?'

The young man ignored him, looking away instead. The goblin struck Father Haven across the face.

'Quiet. Under human. You have been found guilty of hording books and paper, as well as attempting to copy out subversive literature. The penalty is public execution. Death by hanging.'

'Hold on,' said Jonathan. 'There was no mention of death. You said that he would be shunned. No one said that he would be hung.'

The goblin turned to face Jonathan. 'Would you like to take his place, worthy human?' it asked.

The young man shook his head and looked down, hiding his fear and his guilt.

'Jonathan,' called Father Haven. 'Don't worry, lad,' he said. 'I forgive you.'

The goblin struck the priest again. A solid blow that split his bottom lip open. Then he backhanded him with a follow through, splitting open the flesh above his right eye. Blood flowed freely down the priest face and dripped on the floor.

Without warning, Father Haven tore free of the two Orcs and leapt forward, delivering a crushing headbutt to the goblin's nose, crushing it almost flat and thumping the creature to the floor.

'I forgive you, Jonathan,' he shouted again. 'But I don't forgive this evil heathen creature.'

With that the priest disappeared under a flurry of blows from the two Orcs as they smashed him to the ground, kicking and punching him into unconsciousness before they dragged him off to the lock-up, helping the prostrate goblin as they did so.

But Jonathan stayed where he was. Standing in the front room of a small cottage, lit by a single candle.

After a while he found a cloth and used it to wipe up Father Haven's blood.

Then he sat down on the old wooden chair and wept.

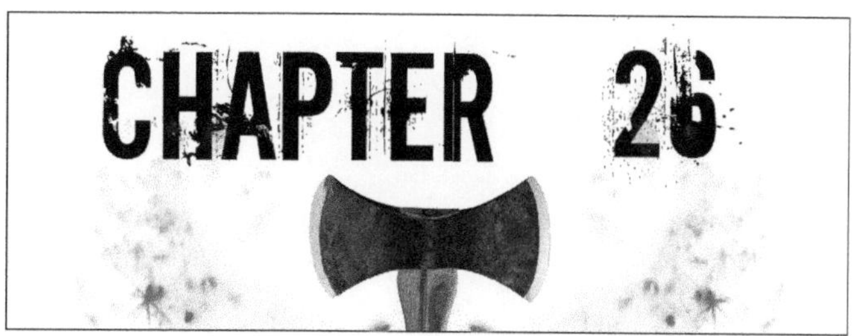

CHAPTER 26

'You cannot simply give yourself up,' said Tad.

'I agree,' added Roo.

'What are my options?' countered Nathaniel.

'Well, for one, don't give yourself up. They are probably going to kill Milly anyway. Let's face it, the Fair-Folk aren't known for their kindness and empathy.'

'Don't say that,' snapped Nathaniel. 'There's no reason for them to kill Milly unless I don't comply.'

'There's no reason not to if you do comply,' continued Tad. 'Anyway, be that as it may, we could threaten them back. Tell them that we declare out-and-out war, see what happens then.'

Nathaniel snorted. 'We're on full alert as it is. We've got six hundred thousand of the buggers breathing down our necks. How many troops do we have?'

Tad shrugged. 'Not exactly sure. Around three hundred thousand.'

'Yep,' agreed Nathaniel. 'And bear in mind that is everyone. Every able-bodied person that we can spare to fight. And they're strung out along the wall, concentrated in the forts. If they hit us with all six hundred thousand at one point, I really do not know how long we could last.'

'We would react. Bring troops from other parts of the wall to reinforce.'

'Fine,' agreed Nathaniel. 'And then if they send another six hundred thousand? And another? You know that they can.'

'I think that, whatever you do,' said Roo. 'They are going to attack. I think that this whole kidnapping thing is a ruse to take you out of the equation, and as soon as they have you either dead or in custody, then they're going to attack.'

The Marine nodded. 'I agree.'

'So,' continued Roo. 'You achieve nothing by giving yourself up. Stay with us. We attack them first, send out the cavalry. Get Papa Dante and his men to sow some discord and sabotage. Take the fight to them. It's the only chance that we have.'

'It's not a bad plan,' agreed Tad.

Nathaniel shook his head. 'No. You guys might not understand this, but I am not going to abandon Milly. I will not let that girl down again.'

Tad leaned forward and looked Nathaniel in the eye. 'Boss, I know that this sounds harsh but, suck it up. You cannot put your guilty feeling about a single girl above the fate of a nation. Of an entire people. The human race. Milly has to be sacrificed. It's a crappy thing to say but that is how it goes.'

The Forever Man smiled and shook his head. 'No, my friend. You've got it all wrong. If I didn't go, if I let that little girl die because of me, then all that we stand for is wrong. If I do that, we will have lost our humanity. And we would have done so without the Fair-Folk's help. Without honor, without dignity, we are less than human. And anyway—who said anything about giving myself up? This is what is going to happen,' continued the Marine. 'I will go. I will go alone, and I will find Milly and bring her back, or I will die trying. That is that—no discussion. You will obey your king. Now, get ready to defend the wall, for, whatever happens, I think that we are all in for a very rough ride.'

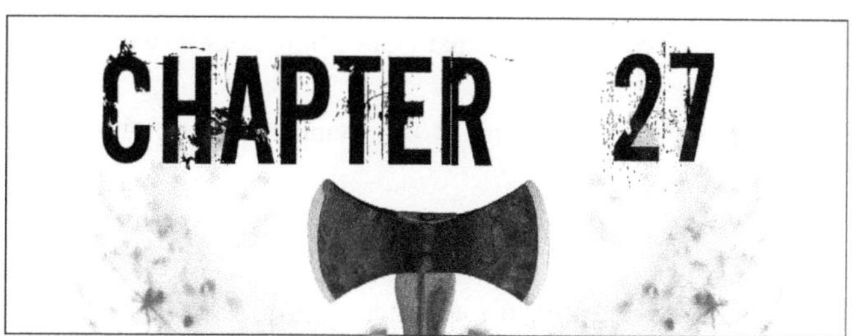

CHAPTER 27

Axel drummed his fingers on the table, hammering out a staccato rhythm born out of frustration. Opposite him sat Jack Olsen and the twins, Donny and Lonny. On their left sat the professor and Father O'Hara.

The prof's head was nodding onto his chest as he wavered between sleep and consciousness. Although the venerable old scholar was still invited to every major meeting, it was now done more as a courtesy than in any hope of worthwhile feedback or constructive advice. The professor was only in his mid-seventies but he had, of late, started to slip slowly into a state of almost permanent dementia. His once magnificent mind now struggled with minor tasks such as reading or remembering where the dining hall was. As well as this, he had started to suffer from major personality changes, becoming suspicious and confused and fearful of strangers.

Father O'Hara was still nominally in charge of the abbey's church and pastoral care for all, but he too had started to slip. His heavy social drinking and late-night carousing had started to take a heavy toll on his liver, not to mention his mental faculties. His eyes had begun to show signs of jaundice and he had started losing weight. But he still had the strength of a bull and the energy of a man half his age, although he had become more aggressive and cantankerous in equal measures.

'Six hundred thousand troops,' reiterated Axel. 'All within a couple of days striking distance of Hadrian's Wall. Have the Fair-Folk said why?'

'They reckon that it's a training exercise,' said Jack. 'Nothing aggressive about it.'

Axel snorted his disbelief. 'They can train anywhere in the country, so why there? No, they're preparing for war. They mean to strike against King

Hogan's Free State. The only thing that I can't figure out is why are they waiting?'

'There are rumors,' said Donny. 'Unsubstantiated, but still quite widespread.'

'What rumors?' asked Axel.

'Sources say that the king's consort has been kidnapped and the Fair-Folk have demanded King Hogan's surrender for her safe return.'

'I wouldn't put much store by that,' denied Axel. 'Nathaniel doesn't have a consort. Nor a wife or girlfriend. And even if he did, he's a leader. He would never put her before the safety of his people.'

'Who is this?' asked the professor.

'King Hogan, Prof,' answered Axel.

The prof nodded. 'Oh, him. Nice man. American wasn't he? Some sort of soldier. I remember him well. Good with an axe. Immortal, I seem to remember … although that doesn't make sense. No one lives forever. Must be thinking of something else.' His head nodded to his chest and he fell asleep.

'So, what now?' enquired Jack.

Axel took a deep breath and then let it out slowly. 'Gentlemen,' he said. 'Whether we like it or not, we are at war. At the moment it is a low-level, cold war. But it is escalating. The Fair-Folk have reduced humanity to little more than draught animals. Menial laborers and serfs. We compete amongst ourselves for food and shelter, social standing, and political gain. Capital punishment has been legislated for even the smallest of crimes. The Fair-Folk have taken away our history, our rights and even our religion.

I think that the abbey is the only small part of the old United Kingdom that still provides some sort of sanctuary from the most draconian of the Fair-Folk rules, but mark my words, that will not last much longer. They mean to declare war on the Free State, and at the same time, or perhaps even before, they will destroy us as well. They can brook no more rebellion, no matter how subtle. So, what to do? I tell you this, when you are at war there are only three options. One, ignore it. Remain neutral like Switzerland in the pre-pulse days. That would be an impossibility. I feel that the Fair-Folk will regard all who are not for them, to be against them. Secondly, one can run. Thirdly—fight.'

Father O'Hara banged his fist on the table, making all except Axel jump in surprise.

'Fight!' he bellowed at the top of his voice. 'If da pig-faces want a fight, well, by God and Jesus we shall give dem one. Fight!'

Axel smiled. 'I agree, Father,' he said. 'But I also counsel running.'

'No,' roared the Irish priest. 'No running. Running is for cowards. We shall fight, and God willing, we shall win.'

'Yes, Father,' agreed Axel. 'We shall fight. But I suggest that we attempt to get the elderly, the women, and the children to safe haven before we start. Sometimes discretion is the greater part of valor, after all, at last estimate the Fair-Folk had two million troops under arms.'

'Fine den,' agreed the irate priest reluctantly. 'Let de bairns and de fogeys go. Den we fight da rest.'

'Fighting someone are we?' enquired the professor.

'Yep,' answered O'Hara. 'We's going to kick de ass of da Fair-Folk. Heathen bastards that they are.'

'Oh, good,' mumbled the prof. 'Never did like them. Odd lot, I say. Will there be soup?'

Father O'Hara looked nonplussed for a moment at the professor's non sequitur, but he rallied well.

'Yes, my old friend,' he assured as he patted the prof's hand. 'Dere will be soup. Lots of soup. As much as you want.'

'Good,' said the professor as his head, once again, slumped to his chest. 'I like soup.'

'Okay, gentlemen,' continued Axel. 'I am going to put together a task force to start the evacuation. We will start by sending small groups out under the cover of night. Final destination, the Free State. I know that it's just as likely to fall as we are, but we have to unite somewhere and that is my choice. Now, to cover our evacuation I want you, Jack, to take all of our guerilla teams and wreak as much havoc as you can on the Fair-Folk and anyone who supports them. That includes the so-called worthy humans and superior humans. Poison wells, burn buildings, dig up roads, lay lethal traps. Kill them, Jack. Kill as many as you can.' Axel turned to Father O'Hara. 'Father, happy with that?'

O'Hara nodded. 'Kill dem all, heathen bastards.' And he took a swig from his ever-present flask of whisky.

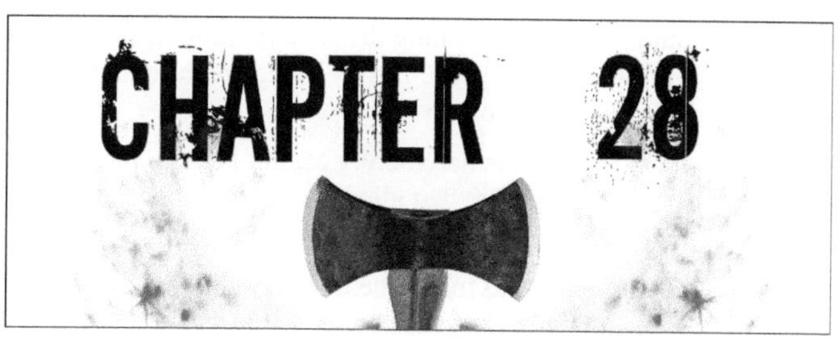

CHAPTER 28

Milly stared out of the window at the frozen stretch of the Thames River. A healthy fire crackled in the large hearth and the walls were adorned with tapestries. Carpets, both old and new, covered the stone floor and her bed, in the far corner of the room, was covered in a mountain of goose-filled eiderdowns.

An eight-seater dining table was covered with the remnants of breakfast. Fish, bacon, sausage, eggs, cheese, and breads. Fresh fruit juice and small beer. The food had been served that morning by Melanie, a plump and happy young human in her early teens. She had obviously been born after the pulse and knew little about the pre-pulse days. She did know that they had been lawless times and there was much war between human and human until the Fair-Folk came and put a stop to all of the violence by bringing law to the land. Milly wanted to talk to her more, ask her questions. Was she happy? What did she think of the Fair-Folk? Had she heard of the Free State? But Melanie had claimed to be too busy and bustled off before Milly could continue her questioning.

On the whole, though, Milly wanted for nothing. A prisoner in the Tower of London. A place once described by historians as, the most luxurious eleventh century palace in the world.

After Orc Sergeant Kob had knocked her out during her kidnapping, she had regained consciousness on the other side of the wall. Kob had treated her firmly but respectfully. He had made it plain that he would not harm her in any way as long as she did not attempt to escape. She had nodded her agreement and then instantly sprung to her feet and sprinted into the forest.

She had been staggered at the ease that the Orc had recaptured her. The Orcs that she had known before had been powerful, thickset creatures. Not clumsy, but stolid and given more to long distance running than bursts of speed. Kob, however, was probably the fastest living creature that she had ever seen. Apart from Nathaniel, of course.

But he had not beaten her. He had merely caught her and then bound her legs together with a piece of leather that allowed her to walk and take normal steps but left her unable to take the longer strides necessary to run.

It had taken them five days to travel the three hundred miles to London. Every morning Kob would wake her with breakfast. Normally fruit or cooked game. Then he would pick her up and run for six hours at high speed. They would stop for a lunch of trail biscuit and then he would carry her again for another six hours. Each evening he would tie her to a tree, hunt some game, cook it, and feed her. The next day would be the same. Three hundred miles in five days while carrying a human being. An effort that transcended superhuman. It was apparent to Milly that Orc Sergeant Kob was a freak amongst Orcs. A super-Orc, superior in every way to his pod-mates.

She had asked him, a few times, how he had become different. To her knowledge, all Orcs were meant to be as close to identical as possible, sticking to an age-old breeding process that had been honed over countless years in order to create the perfect fighting machine. Kob had somehow improved on perfection.

But he had simply shaken his head and said. 'Kob stands alone.'

After a couple of days, she stopped asking.

There was a knock on the door. Judging by the hour she knew that it would be Commander Ammon.

This was her third day in the tower and the commander had visited her twice a day. Each day after breakfast and then again after dinner.

And truth be told, she enjoyed his visits. He was handsome, attentive, and knowledgeable.

He entered the room and smiled. His teeth white against his lightly sun-tanned face. Golden hair flowing to his shoulders, his deep blue eyes twinkled with humor. As he moved towards her his steps were as graceful as a ballet dancer, and he carried his six-foot frame with ease and confidence.

Nathaniel had told Milly, and the rest of the people in the Free State, that the Fair-Folk did not look as the humans perceived them. He claimed that they were actually five-foot high, gray-skinned aliens with no ears, large almond-shaped eyes and thin arms and legs.

Roo had backed up Nathaniel's story although he had slipped in a disclaimer, saying that he could only see the Fair-Folk's true appearance if he saw them in reflection. Milly had stared at Ammon as closely as she could, willing herself to see his 'so-called' true appearance but all she saw was what was in front of her. A six-foot, blond, blue-eyed man.

It was obvious to her that Nathaniel's hatred for the Fair-Folk had driven him to concoct a story about their true looks. A story built out of fear and ignorance and spite. This knowledge worried Milly as it showed her a side of The Forever Man that she had not contemplated before.

Ammon bowed deeply before Milly. 'Greetings, my lady,' he said. 'I trust that all of your desires have been met?'

'Yes,' she replied. 'Thank you, Commander. I was wondering if I could leave the room today. A walk in the fresh air would be most welcome.'

'Alas, my lady,' answered Ammon. 'Your security is of paramount importance, and at the moment, I would prefer it if you stayed in your room.'

'A prisoner?' enquired Milly.

'Nay, lady,' denied Ammon. 'A welcomed guest with, shall we say, a few minor restrictions. You see, Milly, the reason that you are here is so that we have some form of leverage over King Hogan. We desperately desire to talk to him, but he has rejected all of our overtures. We want peace. Peace and prosperity for all, humans and Fair-Folk alike. Separately together we shall forge forward. But King Hogan will not see our side. He has an irrational hatred of the Fair-Folk and our peoples. We know not why as we have ever treated him only with respect and kindness.'

'He merely wants the best for his people,' said Milly.

'Perhaps,' agreed Ammon. 'Or perhaps he simply wants war. He is, from what I have heard, a very powerful man.'

'He is,' affirmed Milly. 'But he can also be gentle and caring and kind. If he has any fault it is that he is too duty bound. He puts his sense of duty before all. Responsibility and obligation are his watchwords, and at all times, he remains true to course regardless of his personal feelings or even the feelings of those close to him.'

'A driven man,' adjudged Ammon. 'Any way, we have informed him that you are here and have assured him that no harm shall come to you as long as he agrees to a personal meeting with me and my peers here, in London.'

Milly shook her head. 'He won't come,' she said. 'He will not put the cause before me. He is not that sort of man.'

'On the contrary,' denied Ammon. 'The man that you have just described to me sounds like the exact sort of man that would give himself up to ensure that no harm came to you.' The commander headed for the door. 'Now, my dear, I have a kingdom to run, so, if all your needs have been fulfilled I shall take my leave.'

'Thank you, Commander,' said Milly. 'Oh,' she added. 'There is one thing. I wonder, could you ask someone to bring me a mirror? There are none in my room.'

Ammon stared at her for a while before he answered. 'Why would you need one, my lady?'

Milly shrugged. 'Female vanity, I suppose. I would like to check my hair. Ensure that I look alright.'

Ammon smiled. 'There is no need, lady,' he assured. 'If you need affirmation of your beauty then you can find it reflected in the eyes of any man who talks to you. I bid you farewell.'

And, with that, the commander bowed and left the room, closing and locking the door behind him as he did so.

Milly thought about his refusal for a while and then decided that she was simply being paranoid. She went and stared out of the window again and wondered if Nathaniel would actually deign to meet with the Fair-Folk. And, if he did, was it a trap or were they genuinely seeking some sort of amicable treaty?

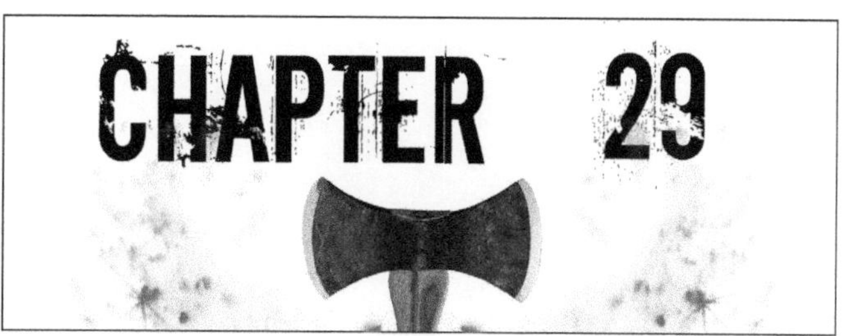

Akimiri Hijiti was the undisputed Hatomoto, or Supreme Warrior of the Annihilators. He stood on the ceremonial plinth and surveyed his fellow Warriors, his compound eyes flickering from side to side as he searched for his three Bushos, High Warriors.

He saw them approaching, walking through the ranks of the Chugan, Standard Warriors. Above them flew flights of Yari, Flying Warriors, swooping back and forth as they scouted the land for any human survivors.

The battle for the possession of the village of Keswick had been extremely unsatisfying. Akimiri had gauged the size of the village and correctly estimated it to house around one thousand humans.

As a result, he had sent in only fifty unblooded Chugan. Novice Warriors. He figured that a twenty to one disadvantage would be large enough to confer honor on the Chugan if they won, but still not so large a disadvantage as to be impossible to overcome.

It had been an unmitigated disaster. Firstly, unlike the Annihilators, the human females and their hatchlings did not fight. Secondly, even the males were not all of the warrior class, some being as feeble and soft as the human women.

In fact, in the end, a mere three hundred human males and a scattering of females had put up any resistance at all. It had been a humiliating experience for his Chugan and both he and they had lost face.

As a result, the next battle that they faced, Akimiri, as Supreme Warrior, would have to ensure that they would face almost insane odds. Anything less than fifty to one would not allow the Chugan to save face and their standing in the hierarchy would suffer greatly.

As it was, the fifty Chugan that he had sent in had already assumed the ritual position of ignominy and they lay, prostrate in front of the ceremonial plinth, their swords unsheathed and plunged into the earth to show that they were no better than farmers, workers of mud and filth. They would remain in this position until given permission to move. And even then, they would be allowed only water to drink and uncooked lentils for sustenance. On top of this it was forbidden for them to communicate with their fellow warriors or even to have eye contact with them. Until the next battle they were considered to be Huzbeki Hitobo or, Shameful Ones. This status would continue until they could be cleansed in worthy battle.

'It is just as well,' said Supreme Warrior Akimiri Hijiti to himself. 'That there will be many, many battles for them to redeem their honor.'

His three Bushos, High Warriors, approached and prostrated themselves in front of him.

'Salutations and felicitations,' they shouted as one. 'May the soul of the warrior be ever yours.'

'And also, yours,' returned Akimiri. 'Now rise and come forward to hear my plans.'

The three Bushos stood and gathered around the Supreme Warrior, standing close in order to hear his further commands.

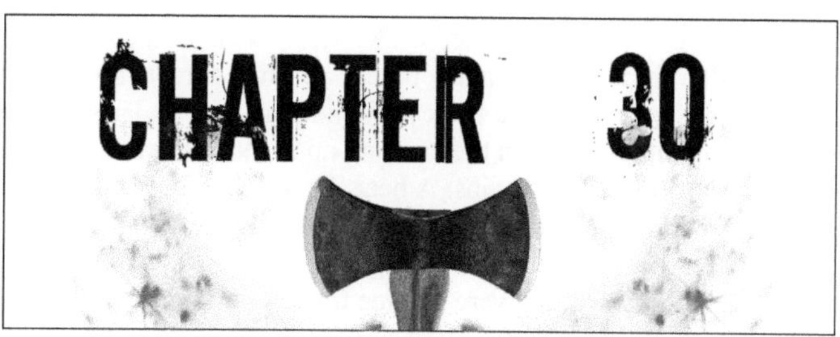# CHAPTER 30

Nathaniel left via a sally port in the main gate. He rode a horse. A good animal, but not a great one. Solid, sturdy, and ugly. Likewise, his clothing was neither ragged nor rich. He wanted to blend in to the local populous. An average man. But still he stood out. For he could not hide his bearing. His pride and strength. His hair flowed in loose curls to his broad shoulders. His dark beard was cropped close to his chin. And his deep green eyes sparkled with excitement. Or perhaps with anticipation.

To those who did not know him, it would not be apparent that he was, The Forever Man. But what was clearly evident was that this was not a man to trifle with.

The Marine heeled the horse into a canter and guided it towards the forest, snow flying from its hooves as it ran, the wind pulling his cloak out behind him like a flag in a stiff breeze.

As he entered the forest he marveled at how it had grown. Once again, the United Kingdom was clothed in beech and oak and fir. He remembered that it had been so during the time of the Picts, before man's insatiable appetite had cleared the trees from the land to make space for wheat and potatoes, grass for dairy farms, and land on which to build.

Now the new trees stood thirty- to forty-feet-high and the boughs spread wide and deep. Packs of wolves roamed freely as did deer and even bears, both black and brown. The bears had escaped from various zoos and circuses, and being the apex predator in the land, their increase in numbers grew rapidly and was unchecked by man.

Using the sun as a guide, The Forever Man rode on in a southerly direction, keeping his eyes open for any sign of habitation, be it human, Orc, or other.

He had ridden for about half a day before he came across the first thing of note. In a clearing amongst the trees were the remains of a large animal. Someone, or something, had torn the creature apart. Nathaniel dismounted and took a closer look at the remains. A bear. Its legs had been hacked off and lay some ten feet from the body. The rest of the carcass was half flayed and the skull had been split in twain with a single blow from what appeared to be a huge broadsword. All around were strange tracks and the Marine recognized them as the Annihilator tracks that Tad had described to him. After carefully studying the spoor and the surrounds, the Marine came to the conclusion that two beings had attacked the bear, or vice versa.

He stood up and shuddered at the thought. Two against a full-grown brown bear. A black bear would have been less frightening as it stood around six foot in height and weighed in at three hundred pounds. But a brown, or grizzly as some called them, stood over nine foot high and weighed in excess of one thousand five hundred pounds. The largest land-based predator in the world.

And two Annihilators had reduced one to a pile of chopped meat with, apparently, no injury to themselves. Nathaniel was under no false illusions. He knew that, if he had to, he could do the same thing to a grizzly himself. But he also knew that he was no ordinary man. The thought of possibly hundreds of these deadly creatures roaming the land filled him with dread.

Knowing that there was little that he could do about it at the moment he mounted up once again and continued on his way, even more vigilant than he had been before.

For the first time in ages the Marine felt at ease. His senses were alert and his eyes roved constantly, but he was free from decisions and drama. Free from the shackles of drama. Free from the shackles of leadership and the bonds of kingship.

He patted his ugly horse on the neck and chuckled to himself. Alone. Not exactly happy but less stressed than usual.

The day drew to a close as the shadows grew full and the sun curtsied its way behind the tree line. Nathaniel pitched camp in his usual manner. Three low walls of snow, a tarpaulin over the top and a small fire at the entrance. He laid a few traps for small game, ate a meal of bread, cheese, and salted ham, and then went to sleep.

The next morning, he beat the sun and was in the saddle as the first pink rays kissed the snowy treetops. In his saddlebags were two dressed rabbits and a squirrel, victims of his night laid traps.

The horse's hooves crunched through the snow as the two of them continued heading south, stopping for a quick lunch, and then carrying on their way.

Two hours before sunset Nathaniel sensed that someone was watching him. He grabbed his axe from its sheath on his saddle and sprung from the horse, rolled into the trees and low bushy cover on the side of the track. The horse simply stopped and stood still.

As he waited a group of six creatures exited the trees opposite him. It was immediately apparent from the descriptions that he had heard that they were Vandals.

Males, small and scrawny with large leathern wings folded in their backs.

The Marine stood up slowly and walked forward in a nonthreatening manner, clipping his axe to his belt as he did so. One of the Vandals came towards him, stopping six feet away and bowing. The others followed suit, bending at the waist, and holding the position until Nathaniel acknowledged them.

'Greetings, friends,' he said.

The one Vandal stood upright. 'Greet-ings. Mast-er.' He beckoned to the others and they stepped forward and each laid a small bundle on the snow. Nathaniel could see that the bundles contained food. Fresh fruit, dried meat, and bread.

'For mast-er,' said the Vandal. Then he pointed at the sky and all around them, turning in a slow circle. 'We watch,' he said. Then he described the arc of the sun, moving his hand back and forth across the sky two times. 'For two suns we will watch. Keep mast-er safe. We warn of dan-ger.'

Then, before Nathaniel could question them, they simply disappeared as they bent the light around themselves and melted back into the cover of the forest.

He picked up the packages and transferred them to his saddlebags, taking out a stick of dried meat to gnaw on as he did so.

Then he saddled up and continued on, feeling slightly more secure knowing that he now had some aerial support. Not quite a Harvest Hawk Gunship or an AH3 Super Cobra. But at least it was something, and every Marine loves air support. Even if he has no idea why it is there.

He made camp that night and feasted on fresh fruit and hard bread, building the fire higher than usual to combat the sudden snap drop in temperature.

The next morning was bedlam. A storm had built up during the night and now the wind howled through the trees, whipping the boughs back and forth and churning the snow up so that it came from all angles.

Nathaniel wasn't sure what time it was as it was still dark with no gleam of sun or moon. Only the faint coruscation of the ever-present pulse-lights glowed faintly from above, washing all with a green graveyard glimmer.

Even in the forest Nathaniel felt exposed. He knew that he had to find a more sheltered place for both himself and his horse. Ignoring the wind and snow as much as possible, he knelt down and placed his hand on the ground, pulling in power and then releasing it, sending it sprawling over the land. Seeking. Finding.

Somewhere to his right. People? Something living. A fairly large group. He took the horses reins and led it in that direction.

The snow filled the air like down, getting in Nathaniel's eyes, ears, and mouth. And the wind battered at him with a primeval force, hammering him. Trying to drive him to his knees.

Eventually, rearing out of the darkness, he saw vague shapes. He trudged towards them, picking the largest one to head to first. As he got within feet of the shape it became apparent that it was a building. Square with thick walls, small shuttered windows, and a thatched roof. In the front, a large double door.

He tried the door, but it was locked so he grasped the heavy iron doorknocker and hammered it down a few times.

Seconds later the door cracked open. Light spilled out and a bearded face stared at him. But before he could say anything the door closed.

He was about to knock again when the door reopened and two young men stepped outside into the storm.

'Welcome, stranger,' said the one. His voice raised in order to be heard above the raging storm. 'Please, go inside. We shall stable your horse and be back shortly.'

Nathaniel nodded his thanks and stepped into the building, shutting the door behind him as he did.

He had obviously found the local tavern or meeting hall. There was a rough bar against the one wall, a large fireplace with roaring fire, and a mixed selection of chairs and tables scattered around the room. Almost all were occupied.

The Marine pulled back the hood of his cloak and upholstered his axe, laying it against the wall next to the door.

'Greetings, all,' he said. 'And my sincere thanks for letting me shelter from the storm. Long has it been since I have come across such bad weather.'

There was a general buzz of greeting and one man, short and thickset, stood and walked towards the Marine, his hand held out to shake.

Nathaniel shook the man's hand, recognizing him as the bearded face that he had first seen at the door when he had knocked.

'I am Taylor,' said the man. 'Mayor and priest of this hamlet. Please, allow me to get you a drink, we have some marvelous ale. Dark and strong.'

Nathaniel grinned. 'Many thanks, Taylor. That would go down a treat.'

He followed the man to the bar and the barman handed over a mug of ale without instruction.

It struck Nathaniel that the dark ale was probably the only drink available in the establishment, but after he had taken an experimental sip, he wasn't bothered by the lack of choice. The beer was excellent. Fruity and bitter with a high alcohol content and an aftertaste of apples.

'It's good,' he said to Taylor. 'Better than good, actually. It's exceptional.'

His statement was greeted by a round of wide grins and Taylor patted him on the shoulder. These were people that were obviously proud of their ale-brewing skills.

'Aye,' said Taylor. 'It's what we do. It's an old Trappist monks' recipe. We call it "Abbey beer." Although it is technically a Trappist beer recipe, we are not a Trappist monastery. Neither are we Trappist monks, so, legally, we aren't allowed to call it Trappist beer. Although we do try our best to adhere to the rest of the production criteria. The brewery must be of secondary importance within the monastery and it should be witness to the business practices proper to a monastic way of life. The brewery is not intended to be a profit-making venture. The income covers the living expenses of the monks and the maintenance of the buildings and grounds. Whatever remains is donated to charity for social work and to help persons in need. And, finally, we constantly monitor our beer to ensure that its quality is beyond reproach, even though the Fair-Folk seem not to have developed a taste for it.'

'Legally?' asked Nathaniel. 'I very much doubt that the Trappist monks are going to descend on you from Belgium and sue for copyright infringement.'

Taylor stared at Nathaniel, his face serious. Not a hint of humor.

'Be that as it may,' he answered. 'Right is right. Just because you can get away with breaking the law doesn't mean that you should.'

The Marine was about to argue that copyright laws and brand infringement didn't actually exist anymore in a world that had been driven back to the same age as when the Trappist monks had originally built their monasteries, but he decided not to. These people had a way of life and who was he to argue against it.

Instead he nodded. 'Very true, Taylor. Very true.' He took another sip of the ale. 'You say that the beer is of secondary importance. What is the primary import of the hamlet?'

'We are a religious order,' said Taylor. 'We live frugally, worship five times a day and try to live a charitable lifestyle. On the whole we keep ourselves separate, only seeing outsiders when we trade our beer. Humans on the whole. We hardly ever see the Fair-Folk or their minions.'

While Taylor was speaking a young woman came over to Nathaniel and offered him a large bowl of soup and a spoon.

'The Marine bowed extravagantly. 'My sincere thanks, good lady,' he said. 'I swear that my stomach was beginning to think that my throat had been cut. Some hot food will be most appreciated.

She laughed and showed the Marine to a seat at a table that had two free places, sitting next to him when he sat down.

Nathaniel picked up his spoon and began to eat. The soup was thick and well spiced, and he ate without talking. While he did so the young woman appraised him openly, without any embarrassment. The rest of the people at the table, two teenage boys and a teenage girl, said nothing. But they too stared at him as he ate.

Finally, after scraping the bowl, the Marine finished his food and sat back in his chair.

'Enough?' asked the woman.

Nathaniel nodded. 'Thank you. My name is Nathaniel.'

The teenagers all giggled out loud and the young woman turned a stern look on them. 'Shush,' she said. 'Watch your manners. The three youngsters looked contrite and bowed their heads.

The woman held out her hand. 'My name is Lorna,' she said. 'Will you be staying with us?'

The Marine nodded. 'If I may. I feel that it would be unwise to venture out with the storm as it is. Perhaps I might be allowed to bed down in the corner here.'

Lorna shook her head. 'Never. You shall stay with me.'

The teenagers giggled again.

Lorna turned on them, this time real anger on her face. 'Go,' she said. 'Leave and go to your homes. We will talk later.'

The three stood up and bowed to Nathaniel and then to Lorna.

'In his name,' they mumbled together.

Lorna nodded her approval. 'Forever in his name,' she reciprocated. 'Now go.'

The scolded teenagers scuttled off, letting in a sharp gust of wind as they let themselves out.

Taylor stood up and tapped a spoon against his mug to attract everybody's attention.

'Time to pray, people,' he stated.

Everyone immediately got off their chairs and knelt on the floor. Nathaniel, not wanting to offend, did the same.

'Let us pray,' said Taylor. 'Forever faithful are we.'

'And he shall live forever,' intoned the congregation.

'Alpha and Omega shall he be.'

'Eternal and everlasting,' whispered the people.

'By the power of the light eternal and the power everlasting, he shall grant us strength.'

'Unending and timeless is his wisdom.' 'Forever is his name,' spake Taylor.

'Forever is his name,' repeated the congregation.

'We shall now spend five minutes in silent contemplation,' said Taylor. 'Let us bow our heads.'

Nathaniel sat in silence and let his mind wander back. He remembered his mother and father. His family. Particularly his sister. None of them had ever been very close. He had joined up as soon as he had left school, and although he had kept in touch with his parents and siblings, he had missed birthdays and christenings. Graduations and anniversaries. The Marine Corps had become his family. Like all Marines he gave an oath to God, country, and Corps. But also, like all Marines, corps often came before all. Semper Fidelis as the motto went. Forever faithful.

Nathaniel frowned as a thought brushed across his consciousness, but before he could pin it down, Taylor stood up and the people started talking amongst themselves, destroying his train of thought.

He sat back down at the table. Lorna brought him another beer and he sipped at it whilst all around him people chatted. Their conversations were trivial. But not meaningless. They spoke of crop rotation and livestock. Of beer and hops and wheat. Sugar made from beets and the need to fix a leak in the water tower.

It was infinitely relaxing. There was no need to think of tactics, no military decisions. No thought of taxation nor medical help for the people. No raiders, no Annihilators. A wave of jealousy washed over the Marine before he quashed it mercilessly. He laughed inwardly at himself. All of this peace and quiet was all well and good but he knew, in his heart of hearts, that it would be a few more days before he hankered for action.

He picked up his beer and noticed that it had been refilled so he took a deep draught.

Lorna stood up and took him by the hand. 'Come,' she said. 'It's getting late.'

The Marine stood up and followed her. She stopped momentarily to bid Taylor goodnight.

'By your leave, holy man,' she said.

He nodded. 'Forever in his name, child.'

Nathaniel followed Lorna from the hall and into the howling storm. It was a short walk to her cottage, but if she had not been with him, the Marine would easily have gone astray, such was the violence of the snowstorm.

She opened her front door and the two of them bundled into the room, slamming the door behind them as quickly as they could. Nathaniel noted that the door was unlocked and mentioned it.

'We are too isolated to worry about strangers stealing from us and the locals would never stoop so low. We are like family.'

Lorna placed some kindling on the low embers that sat in her fireplace and blew it to flame, adding some heavier logs on as soon as the blaze rose up. Within minutes the room was well lit by the dancing orange flames and the cold was driven back as the room filled with heat. It was a small cottage. A single room with a door leading to the bathroom. An alcove for cooking, an old sofa, and a single bed. The bed was piled high with cushions and blankets.

Without talking the young woman pulled the cushions and blankets off the bed and lay them down in front of the fire. Then she stripped her clothes off, folded them and laid them neatly on the back of the sofa.

She turned to face the Marine, her body a symphony of curves and shadows as the light from the fire flickered across her naked skin, painting it in a wash of oranges and pinks and reds.

She tilted her head to one side and smiled. 'Come on,' she urged. 'Your turn. Or are you too shy?' she joshed.

Nathaniel blushed and then grinned. 'No,' he denied. 'Not shy ... just ...'
He shrugged and then disrobed. Throwing his garments onto the floor next to
the sofa and kicking his boots into the corner.

Lorna stared at his nakedness with an expression akin to awe.

His dark hair tumbled to his shoulders and his face was framed with his
customary short-cropped beard. His shoulders tapered down in a wedge shape
to his slim waist and the muscles of his thighs stood out like corded ropes
wrapped in velvet.

Barely an inch of his body wasn't scarred in some way or another. The
scars were all well healed but still visible. Long ragged slashes of sword cuts,
short indented knife scars and the dimpled puckers of bullet wounds. Muscles
of whipcord and steel stretched across his chest and shoulders and his
abdominals stood out like two rows of pebbles on a beach of white sand.

She took a step towards him and his arms enveloped her and held her
tight.

And outside the wind howled and screamed its fury.

***

When Nathaniel woke the next morning, it was to the sound of the never-
ending storm. The wind still thumped at the shutters and doors and the sun
was a mere suggestion peering through the complete whiteout.

Lorna had already risen and dressed. She brought him a hot cup of herbal
tisane, sweetened with honey. He sat up and sipped at it. It was good. A blend
of dried dandelion, hibiscus, and ginger.

After he had finished, he stood up and got dressed. 'What now?' he
asked.

'Communal prayer,' answered Lorna. 'At the hall. Then we can stay on
or come back. There will be no work whilst the storm rages.'

The Marine nodded. 'Okay. You guys sure do a lot of praying.'

'Does that bother you?' asked Lorna.

Nathaniel shook his head. 'No. I believe in God. As far as my worshipping has gone I have slipped, but I reckon that He's got bigger things to worry about than my piety.'

Lorna smiled. 'So, you follow the old religion?'

Nathaniel raised an eyebrow. 'As opposed to?'

'Well,' said Lorna. 'We don't follow the old Judeo-Christian myths. As a group, we figure that the appearance of the Fair-Folk and their Orcs pretty much disproves the old Christian legends. If there was a god and we were created in his image, then what are Orcs? Or goblins? No—we follow the new religion. It is small at the moment, but it is gathering momentum. And that is as it should be, because forever faithful are we.'

'Semper Fidelis,' said Nathaniel.

'What?'

He shook his head. 'Nothing. Tell me more about this new god.'

'Alpha and Omega shall he be,' said Lorna. 'Eternal and everlasting and Forever shall be his name.'

The Marine grasped the back of the sofa for support. 'You gotta be joking,' he croaked. 'Are you talking about The Forever Man?'

Lorna's face lit up. 'You have heard of him?' she asked joyfully.

Nathaniel nodded. 'You could say that. Yeah.'

'So, you know that he is immortal? He has been created by the universe to guide humanity and return us to our former glory. He brings with him the light and the truth and he is capable of great and powerful magiks. It is said that he is a giant, standing head and shoulders above the tallest of men, and that he can travel through time at will, and even as we speak, he is in all places at the same time, guiding and controlling. Even here his influence can be felt.'

'Especially here,' agreed the Marine.

'So, you believe?' asked Lorna.

Nathaniel nodded. 'Yes. Intimately. Not sure about him being so big, though. And all that other stuff sounds a little exaggerated.'

Lorna shook her head. 'Please don't talk like that, Nathaniel. It sits too close to blasphemy for my comfort. Question not your faith. Simply believe and you shall be rewarded.'

'Do you mind if I stay here?' enquired the Marine.

'You would prefer to pray alone?' asked Lorna. 'To spend some time alone with your god?'

Nathaniel nodded. 'Umm … yep. In a manner of speaking.'

'Of course,' agreed Lorna. 'I shall be back in half an hour.'

The young woman closed the door behind her as she left.

Nathaniel collapsed on the sofa.

'A god,' he whispered to himself. 'If Tad were here now he would laugh his socks off,' the Marine continued talking to himself as he attempted to get his head around the current information.

He took a deep breath. 'I must tell them.' Then he laughed to himself as he envisaged breaking the news. 'Hi. That god that you all worship … well … actually that's me. Tah Dah!' Nathaniel snorted. 'Bloody ridiculous, that's what that is.'

He stood up and went over to the kitchen area where he made himself another cup of tisane. It wasn't as good, as he had no real idea on what quantities of each dried ingredient to put in. 'Some sort of god I am,' he muttered to himself. 'Can't even make a decent cup of tea.'

He sat back down with his bitter brew and thought hard. He could use magik to convince them. He could fight them. He could get someone to stab him through the heart and show them his immortality.

Or he could simply wait for the storm to blow itself out and then leave. After all, they were an isolated group in the middle of nowhere and there was little chance that their weird religion would grow to any appreciable size.

The door opened, and Lorna let herself in, shaking the snow from her jacket as she did so. She placed a loaf of bread and a hunk of cheese on the table in the kitchen alcove.

'Here,' she said. 'Eat.'

Nathaniel smiled and shook his head. 'Not that hungry at the moment.'

'I don't care,' said the young woman. 'You'll need to keep your energy up.'

'Why?' asked the Marine.

Lorna smiled and started taking her garments off.

Nathaniel hacked off a large slice of bread and cheese and bolted it down before he too stripped off once again.

And outside the storm continued unabated, pummeling the small cottage with snow and sleet and ice.

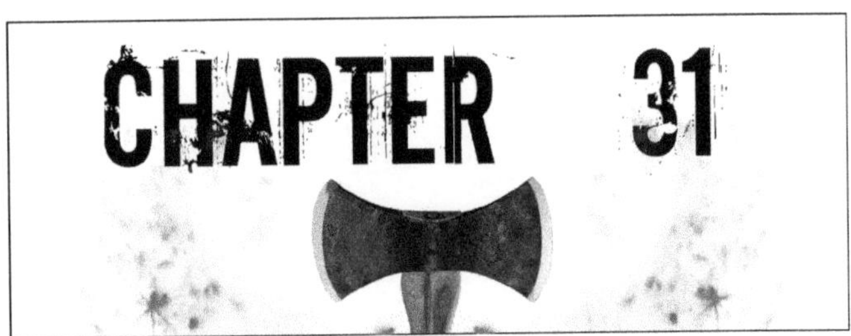

CHAPTER 31

Tad craned his neck back as he watched the masses of Vandals flying in. There were more than five thousand in the air, and massed on the parade ground behind him, there stood another ten thousand plus.

The little big man was amazed in their numbers, as he had suspected that there would be perhaps a thousand or so of the skinny flying creatures. But such was their skill at remaining unseen that he had vastly underestimated their presence.

Chief Char-rek of the Vandals stood next to Tad and watched his people fly in.

The massed flyers reminded Tad of old black-and-white movies of World War II during the Battle of Britain when the English skies had been filled with both British and Nazi fighter planes and bombers.

And, like the olden day flights of Spitfires, the Vandals flew in V-shaped formations of ten or twenty, wheeling above them in stacked layers, waiting to land.

All around the parade ground stood hundreds of humans, watching wide-eyed as the new alien creatures shuttled in.

Roo strode over and tipped his hat in greeting to Tad and the chief.

'G'day,' he said. 'Impressive, isn't it?'

Tad nodded his agreement. 'I had no idea that there were so many of them.'

'Used to be many more,' said chief Char-rek. 'War with the Annihilators dim-inished our numbers. Be-fore, the Vandal race would block out the sun. Now we are mer-ly a small cloud. Still, we can-not stand idly by. We have come to assist hu-mans. To fight alongside. For time long before we have fought the Enemy. They have de-feated us. We fled. Using the power of the source-light we opened a gate and we ended up here. But now they have followed. So, we fight again. You fight. We are to-gether.'

Roo, Tad, and Char-rek stood and watched for a while longer as the rest of the Vandals continued to land, then the chief went to organize their dispersal and to show them where to set up camp.

Roo had put aside an area next to the river for the Vandals but they had asked to be moved away and into the forest. It seemed as though they were happier if they could conceal themselves, using both their light-bending abilities and screens of natural camouflage to do so.

Chief Char-rek had been in contact with Tad via his emissary, Grim-son the scout and together they had decided on an arrival date for the flying creatures to arrive.

True to their word they had started landing at sun up on the agreed date. By that evening the entire Vandal community was ensconced in the forest and their concealment skills were such that there was not a single sign of the over seventeen thousand inhabitants.

That night, Roo, Tad, and chief Char-rek stayed up until the small hours discussing and planning their next moves.

Many more reports of the Annihilators had been coming in, the Fair-Folk and their Orcs were camped in close proximity to the wall, and The Forever Man was incognito somewhere between the wall and London.

War was drawing closer and all that Tad could do was tread water as best he was able to until their leader returned.

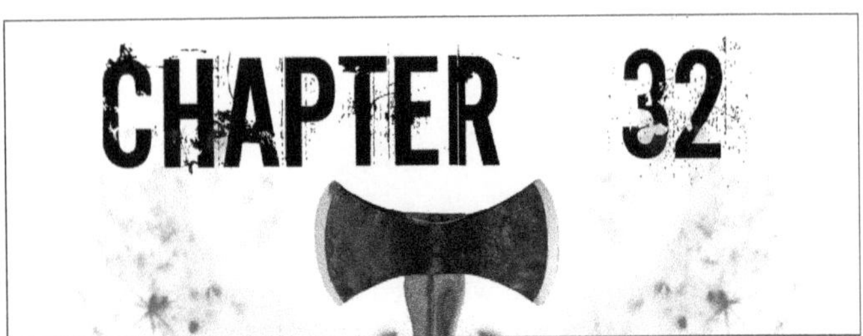

The storm had abated somewhat. Downgraded itself from a howling blizzard to a merely unpleasant weather pattern.

The snow still fell, and the wind howled but it was more petulant than vicious. A tantrum as opposed to an act of violence.

Nathaniel had left early that morning. He had bid Taylor and Lorna goodbye and had given them his thanks. There was no awkwardness in his leaving and they seemed pleased that he shared their view that The Forever Man existed. The Marine had decided not to enlighten them any further regarding his actual identity. After all, he figured that their relative isolation, and the mere fact that considering him as a god was total loony tunes, would prevent the cult from expanding.

He made good time considering the storm. At least the inclement weather had some advantages, he did not expect to see, nor did he, any Orc patrols. Like most in the military, the Orc sergeants kept patrols to a minimum during foul weather.

Four days later, as the sun was setting, he found himself in the area around Nottingham. He had been following the old M1 motorway, merely in order to help with his direction. The old road itself was as rough to travel on as the open ground next to it. At times even more so. He had kept a keen eye out for Orc patrols and had so far come across only one, and it had been easily avoided by simply melting in to the forest and laying low until they passed.

Up ahead he saw a wash of smoke rising into the blustery sky and he headed towards it, hoping for a little company, some local news, an indoor room for the night and perhaps some bread to supplement his diet of game. But as he got closer to the small village he could see that it was mean and poor. The thatch on the roofs was patchy and ragged as a beggar's beard and the fences lay broken and untended.

Undeterred, the Marine trudged down the main pathway to what appeared to be a central hall or pub of sorts. He hitched his horse to a post that was situated under a covered lean-to next to the building. Then he covered him with a blanket, unclipped his axe and his saddlebags from the saddle and went to the front door.

He noticed, with surprise, that the windows were barred with strong metal rods and the door was locked and bound with steel straps. He knocked using the doorknocker and waited. After a while a small viewing flap opened in the center of the door and someone peered out at him. There was another short pause and then the door was opened, and a short, skinny man ushered the Marine inside.

'Come on,' he grunted. 'Move it. It's not safe out there. They come out after the sun goes down.'

Nathaniel hesitated. 'What about my horse?'

The man shook his head. 'Don't be stupid,' he said. 'They don't touch the livestock.'

The Marine had no idea what the man was talking about, but he entered the building nonetheless, closing the door behind him as he did. The short man double-locked it and drew a stout wooden bar across.

Nathaniel found himself in a tavern room. A fire smoked away in the corner. The chimney obviously needed cleaning, so it wasn't drawing well. More than half of the smoke drifted into the room causing a blue-white fug so thick as to inhibit sight.

There were only another four people in the room. A man standing behind the bar, the skinny man that had just let the Marine in, an old-timer with an outrageously long white beard, and a woman of middle age. Dark-eyed with a thatch of auburn hair that looked as though it hadn't seen a brush for over a decade.

'Greetings,' said the Marine.

All that he received in reply was a collection of suspicious stares.

Eventually the man behind the bar spoke.

'You're not from around here,' he said. His voice devoid of emotion. Dead. Defeated.

'I am not,' agreed Nathaniel. 'I hail from up North. Beyond the wall.'

'No one lives beyond the wall,' argued the bartender to a general nod of agreement from the other three occupants of the room.

'Well, that can be your little secret then,' retorted Nathaniel. 'Nevertheless, that's where I come from. So, tell me,' he continued. 'Why the security and the less than hearty welcome?'

The skinny man sniffed wetly before he spoke. 'That would be on account of the ghouls,' he said.

'Ghouls?'

The man nodded. 'Aye, ghouls. Skinny, white as snow, pointed teeth. They feed on human flesh, particularly children. Ghouls.'

'They only come out after sunset,' added the woman. Her voice was deep and husky and smooth as velvet. A complete contrast to her craggy, worn exterior.

'I've never heard of ghouls actually existing,' said Nathaniel.

'Lots of things that I never heard of,' returned the skinny man. 'That don't mean they don't exist.'

'How long have they been here?'

Skinny shrugged. 'Long time. Always, perhaps.'

'Why don't you leave?' asked Nathaniel. 'Or do something about it?'

'We've always lived here,' affirmed the skinny man. 'And what could we do?' asked the woman. 'They're supernatural. They make no sound and leave no trace. They ghost in like wraiths. White will-o'-the-wisps. There's nothing that we can do. And they only come out at night. So, we hide. We lose someone every now and then, but it's no worse than anywhere else in the world.'

'Aye,' confirmed the skinny man. 'Better the devil you know.'

'Are they out there now?' asked the Marine.

Everyone nodded.

'More than likely,' confirmed the woman.

Nathaniel stood up. 'I think that I'll go and take a look,' he said as he walked over to the door, picking his axe up as he did so. 'Never seen a ghoul before.'

The occupants of the tavern looked at him blankly.

Eventually the skinny man shrugged. 'It's your funeral,' he said. 'Just make sure that you leave quick. I'll lock the door behind you and then you're on your own. Can't let you back in. Couldn't take the risk.'

Nathaniel nodded his acceptance of the man's terms. 'Fair enough,' he said as he opened the door and stepped out.

The skinny man slammed the door shut behind him and the Marine heard the sound of the lock turning and the bar being slid home.

The Marine looked around. The light of the gibbous moon reflected off the white snow and cast more than enough light to see well. He walked around the corner to his horse. The animal snorted a greeting and Nathaniel patted its neck.

'Hello, ugly horse,' he said, checking that the blanket was still covering his back. Then he pulled a feedbag from the saddle and filled it with oats from his pack, finally attaching it to ugly horse's nose so that it could eat.

'Seen any ghouls?' he asked the beast.

Horse chomped away at its bag of oats and didn't react to the question.

The Marine pulled his cloak tight around him and then he swung the axe over his shoulder as he trudged through the village, peering down alleyways, and looking out into the surrounding forest.

As he walked he wondered what he was doing. What misguided sense of duty had caused him to elect to traipse about in the dark looking for a demon with rows of sharp teeth and a penchant for human flesh?

If he were inclined to be kind to himself, he would have supposed that he was out in the dark in order to protect the innocent people hiding from the ghouls. But if he was totally honest he would admit that he was less than inclined to protect them. Deep down he wondered why they hadn't done something themselves. And if they were too scared to react forcibly then why did they not simply move. It wasn't as if there was a massive shortage of spare housing or land in the new world.

But the more that he thought about it, the more obvious the answer became. People feared change. Even change for the better.

Entropy was a powerful force and its gradual decline into disorder was often irreversible.

He had been outside for almost an hour when he got his first glimpse. A white figure, thin and ethereal, flittered across his vision. As he spun to watch it another ghosted after it. And then another. Three pale wraiths, slipping through the snowflakes, bathed in moonlight, as quiet as figments of the imagination.

The Forever Man brought his axe to port and ran after them. His footsteps were as cotton upon snow. Unheard. Stealthy beyond those of mere mortals. Otherworldly.

The eerie trio stopped outside a small cottage, peering in at a badly shuttered window. Scratching on the glass. Snickering and grunting.

From inside Nathaniel could hear mewls of terror.

He stopped directly behind the three specters and held his axe high.

'Hey, ghoul dudes,' he called. 'Time to party.'

As one they turned on him, their mouths open wide, their teeth were sharp as needles. Yellow and stained. Their breath stank of rotting flesh.

The axe sang its song. Slicing through snowflakes and necks. Sleet and limbs. A sibilant hissing melody of death and destruction. Of blood and desire. Retribution.

For The Forever Man was the judge eternal and he had brought down his gavel upon the sinners.

Blood stained the snow in a wash of bright red as the three beings fell to the ground, hacked through and through again.

Real blood. Human blood.

The Forever Man picked up a severed head by its hank of lank greasy hair and he stared at it.

The lips were peeled back in a grimace of rigor and it became immediately apparent that it was human. Its teeth sharpened to points by file or chisel. Its skin was pale, and it was thin to the point of emaciation, every muscle in its jaw standing out like a chart in a biology lesson.

The so-called wraiths were no more than tribalistic cannibals.

Nathaniel kicked at the body that lay curled up in the snow at his feet. Then he knelt down and pulled the flowing white tunic off the corpse before standing back up and heading to the tavern.

He stood outside the tavern door and banged loudly. 'Hey,' he shouted. 'Open up. It's me.'

There was a pause before someone answered, their voice muffled by both the door and the weather.

'Who is, me?' they asked.

'The stranger,' answered Nathaniel. 'From up north, beyond the wall. I think that I've sorted out your ghoul problem. Let me in.'

Again, there was a long pause.

'No can do, stranger,' said the voice. 'After all, how do we know that you're alone?'

'Or what if you've been possessed by the ghouls?' asked another voice.

The Marine reined in his impatience before he spoke again. 'Don't be stupid,' he urged. 'Open the door.'

'No!'

'Last chance,' said Nathaniel.

'Or what?' asked the voice. 'You'll bash the door in? Three inches of solid oak and a steel locking bar—I don't think so. We'll just wait until sunrise if that's alright with you.'

The Forever Man didn't even bother to use his magikal powers. No fireballs. No lightning. He merely lifted his foot up to his chest and unleashed it, hammering into the middle of the door, and literally tearing it off its hinges and smashing it into the middle of the room.

'Knock knock, morons,' he said as he walked inside and plunked the severed head down on the bar. He lay the white tunic down next to it, stood back and gestured with a sweep of his arm. 'Behold. A dead ghoul.'

The woman with the husky voice took one look and slid off her chair in a dead faint.

'They're just people,' continued Nathaniel. 'Malnourished, sharpened teeth, floaty white tunic. Simply people. You guys have been living in terror for nothing.'

The skinny man shook his head, his features ashen with fear.

'No,' he said. 'They only become flesh when you kill them. They're ghouls.'

'Whatever,' argued Nathaniel. 'You hit them with an axe and they die.'

He poked at the white tunic. It was a simple cotton coat, at least twenty years old, worn thin by countless washings, its hemline ragged and frayed. Something about it looked familiar but he couldn't quite place what. He lent forward and picked it up. All of a sudden, he knew what it was. A white doctors' coat.

And he remembered.

Nottingham. The Barnet House Psychiatric Hospital. Doctor Henry Luckman. Long pork. Doctors and nurses eating their patients.

He had left them. Faced with exterminating the staff and letting the patients starve to death he had gone with what he thought was the lesser evil. He had figured that the patients would at least have some semblance of life before they were culled for the pot.

And his decision had caused over two decades of fear and degradation to an entire collective of innocent people.

He walked behind the bar and helped himself to a bottle of whisky, pulling the cork with his teeth and slugging down a long pull. The barman was about to say something, but seeing the look on the Marine's face, he decided upon discretion instead.

Nathaniel walked over to a table, sat down, and drank some more of the rough spirits, seeking to quench the fire of guilt and anger that roared in his belly.

In the meantime, the old man who had been sitting quietly in the corner, picked up the ruined door and propped it up in the doorway, blocking a substantial proportion of the inclement weather. Then he went over to the woman who had passed out and rubbed her wrists until she came to. He gave her a sip of his drink and helped her to her seat.

No one ventured outside, and no one dared talk to Nathaniel who sat at his table, swigging from his bottle, on his face an expression of barely contained rage.

The inhabitants of the tavern sat in uncomfortable silence for almost an hour.

And then The Forever Man stood, picked up his axe, grabbed his saddlebags and headed for the door, kicking it aside as he left. He turned and gave the company one last look. 'By the end of tomorrow, you shall no longer be troubled by these things,' he said. 'I am sorry, but I will make it right.'

He untied his horse, mounted up and rode off.

The skinny man pushed the door back into place once again.

'Why did he apologize?' he asked the room in general.

The old man shrugged, as did the rest of the occupants.

'That is one very scary man,' said the husky-voiced woman as she summed up everyone's thoughts in a single sentence.

There was a general mumbling of agreement.

The barman covered the severed head with the white tunic and then he served a round of fresh drinks—on the house.

***

The weather and the lack of light made the tracks difficult to follow but Nathaniel conjured up a ball of blue-white fire to help him see and he walked alongside his horse, peering closely at the signs.

The job was made slightly easier by the fact that the imitation ghouls had made no attempt to cover their tracks. Scuffled footprints, broken twigs and crushed leaves lay liberally along their chosen pathway, and to someone with Nathaniel's tracking skills, this was as a painted arrow pointing the way.

Eventually, as the sun was rising, he came across the remnants of a high chain-link fence, unraveled through neglect and the ravages of time. He rode through a gap, keeping his eyes open.

After a few minutes he saw it. Time had taken its toll, but ostensibly, the building had not changed.

A huge Victorian edifice done in a Gothic revival style. All red brick, mullioned windows, cupolas, and round roof turrets. Unlike the first time that he had seen it, the building was now covered in thick ivy and many of the windows were broken. The front door, however, was still intact and the ground floor windows had all been boarded up.

There was no sign of life.

He tethered ugly horse to a low hanging branch and walked up to the front door, his axe ready to swing.

The door was barred from the inside. He slid the blade of his axe through the doorjamb and levered the bar up, pushing the door open as he did so.

The inside was thick with dust and detritus. The smell of mold and rotting meat permeated the air. Little light made it through the shutters and what did showed tracks across the floor. Passages through the dust, showing where people walked most frequently.

As he wandered down the main corridor memories flooded back to him. The meal that he had eaten, thinking that it was pork, only to discover later that he had eaten the flesh of another human being. His outrage at the doctor and the staff. His helpless inability to do anything about it.

His ultimate failure.

He heard sounds coming from a room at the end of the long dark corridor and he hurried forward. Someone was giggling. Laughing. Someone else was moaning. A long drawn out wail. There was no real urgency to the sound. No pain. No fear. It seemed simply to be an outpouring of random gloom. A formless lamentation.

The Marine pushed the door open and walked in.

There were seven people in the room. Six wraith-like humans. Sharpened teeth, graveyard pallor. Dressed in old white doctors' coats.

Behind a huge scarred wooden desk sat a man barely recognizable as the one doctor Henry Luckman that Nathaniel had met and despised so many years before. The two decades had treated Luckman with the distain due to such a horror of a human being. His hair hung in lank twists from his half bald pate. His stomach was hugely distended, even though his limbs and neck were chicken-skinny. His eyes, although hidden deep in his sockets, glinted with an insanity that was palpable across the room and his hands shook with a violent palsy.

The human wraiths hissed and capered about the room, snapping at Nathaniel as he walked forward. But they kept their distance, ensuring that they did not come within striking distance of his terrible axe.

A barracuda swimming through a shoal of bait fish.

A leopard amongst jackals.

Luckman glared insanely at The Forever Man and then he burst out laughing.

The human wraiths stared at their master's mirth, and in obedience, they joined in, except for the one that returned to wailing tonelessly in lamentation.

Nathaniel stood amongst the insane cacophony and said nothing.

'I know you,' said the doctor. 'You haven't changed. You're the same age. Have you travelled forward in time?' He rubbed his eyes with the backs of his hands. 'They've sent you to get me, haven't they?'

'Who?' asked Nathaniel.

'Them,' replied the doctor. 'All of them. They're jealous, you see. Rotten with envy.'

Nathaniel recognized the doctor's symptoms immediately. The hugely distended stomach, the uncontrollable shaking, the rampant paranoia.

'You have Prions disease,' said the Marine.

'What?' shouted Luckman. 'So now you're the doctor? Do you even know what Prions disease is?'

'Human mad cow,' answered Nathaniel. 'You get it from eating other people. You get it from being a cannibal.'

The doctor sighed. 'Oh God, that again. Every time that I see you it's all that you talk about. You're fixated on cannibalism. It's boring. Boring, boring, boring.'

Luckman stood up and pointed a shaking finger at the Marine. 'And I am afraid that the penalty for being boring is death. Kill him!' he screeched.

The wraiths gathered around the Marine, hissing and spitting like wild cats, looking for an opportunity to lunge forward. To bite. To rend. To eat.

'I think not,' said The Forever Man. The axe spun.

They were fast. And as agile as animals. But The Forever Man was infinitely faster than them. Waves of heat boiled off him as he swung and ducked and rolled. The axe sang its joy as it hewed flesh from bone. All about him the room was covered in thick red blood.

And then he stood before the doctor.

'I should have done this when we first met,' said Nathaniel.

'Wait,' the doctor threw his hand up. 'Don't do this. It's not my fault. I only did what anyone else would have done in my situation. Please. I implore you. Let me live.' He giggled. As high-pitched and breathy as a little girl. 'Let the doctor live,' he simpered. 'Let him live.'

The axe swung in a tight circle. Luckman's head leapt from his shoulders like a frightened animal escaping a trap. It hit the wall and bounced back to land at the Marine's feet.

Nathaniel looked down at it for a while and then he kicked it under the desk.

'Asshole.'

***

The Forever Man sat on his ugly horse and stared at the conflagration that had consumed the Barnet House Psychiatric Hospital. A pyre that he had caused.

After he had dispatched the doctor he had roamed the rooms and the corridors like the angel of death himself. Killing all that crossed his path and then conjuring up balls of flame to consume the rest.

He had forever cleansed the evil of that place, scoured it from living memory and burned away its very existence. And there was no way that it could ever return.

Using his heels to spur his horse on, the Marine continued towards London.

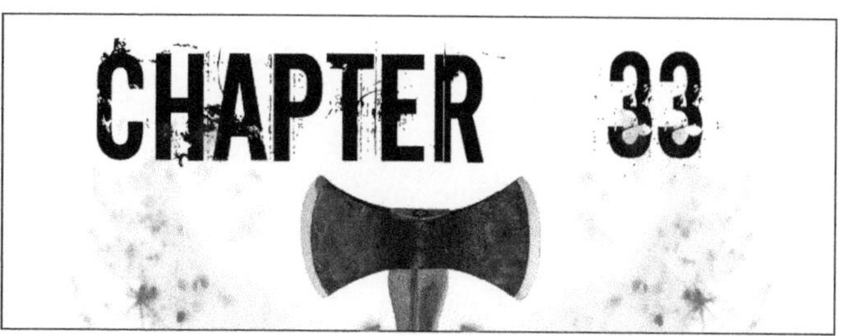

CHAPTER 33

Personally, Tad was not that convinced about the threat of the Annihilators. But chief Char-rek was absolutely certain that it was only a matter of time before vast amounts of the insectoid creatures attacked the humans.

As a result of his conviction, he insisted that the Vandals be incorporated into the human free folk military in order for Tad, Roo, and the chief to formulate a coherent use of air support to strengthen the army.

Tad was more than happy to oblige because, even though he remained unconvinced regarding the Annihilators, he was more than sure that the Fair-Folk would be attacking in the near future.

Due to the Vandals' abhorrence of steel, chief Char-rek told Tad that their normal way of fighting was fairly simple. Mainly, they gathered a sack of large rocks, as many as each individual could comfortably fly with, and then they went high and simply dropped them on their opponents. This was usually followed up by a ground assault involving bronze swords and bronze-tipped spears.

If and when they ever came up against other flying adversaries they fought it out in the air, hand-to-hand.

Both Tad and Roo grinned when they heard this. They both instantly knew that, with a little effort, they could raise the aerial efficiency of the Vandals to a whole new level.

The first thing that they did was to replace the sacks of rocks with bundles of short, bronze-tipped arrows. Each bolt was around a foot long with a four-inch, leaf-shaped, razor-sharp head. After a few experiments they worked out that the average Vandal could fly easily with a bundle of twenty bolts.

Secondly, Roo designed a simple, small, double-bowed, pistol crossbow. This light weapon was capable of firing two consecutive bronze bolts at a lethal distance of up to fifteen yards. They were easy to manufacture and Roo got all available blacksmiths, carpenters, handymen, and their assistants onto churning them out, thereby increasing the Vandals' hand-to-hand combat capabilities by a huge factor.

Out of the seventeen thousand or so Vandals, chief Char-rek deemed that eight thousand were capable of combat. Tad reckoned that it would be a while until they had made enough weapons and munitions for the entire Vandal wing.

After a few days, however, the free people had made more than enough drop arrows to allow a few practice runs and so it was that Char-rek and another five hundred Vandals took to the skies, each carrying a bundle of twenty arrows.

Tad organized a hundred man-sized hay bales to be scattered about an open field for target practice and the Vandals flew high over the target, mere specks in the sky, where they released their payload.

The exercise was an unqualified success. Ten thousand heavy, broad-bladed arrows plummeted to earth at a velocity of over 250 miles per hour. On their journey down, they spread out to cover an area of roughly one hundred feet square. This resulted in a density of one arrow every square foot.

Tad clapped Roo on the back. 'Deadly,' he said.

Roo laughed. 'Not exactly precision bombing, but it'll do.'

The target area looked like a giant's pincushion. Every hay bale had at least three or four arrows embedded deeply in it. Had they been actual living creatures the effect would have been catastrophic.

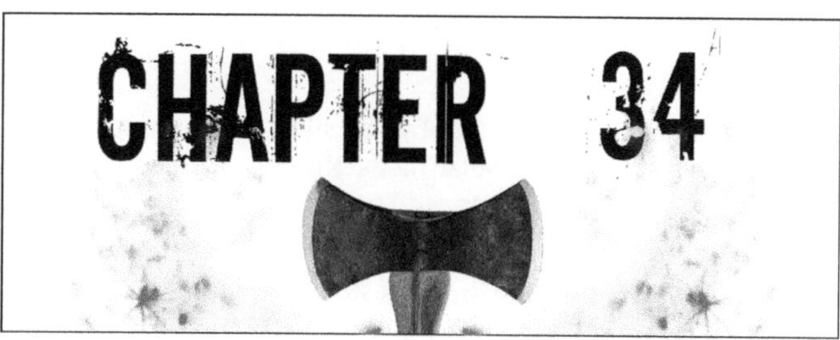

CHAPTER 34

Orc Sergeant Kob whipped his wooden practice sword around his body and connected with the Orc opposite him, striking him in the chest and knocking him to the ground. Then he leapt over the prostrate body, and using the pommel of his practice sword, dealt a knockout blow to his second opponent. Both the third and the fourth were knocked to the floor with a sidekick and a vicious headbutt.

Kob shook his head in disappointment. He had handpicked four of the very best combatants that he could find, and once again, they were no match for him.

He ignored them, dropped the wooden sword to the ground and left the courtyard, deep in thought.

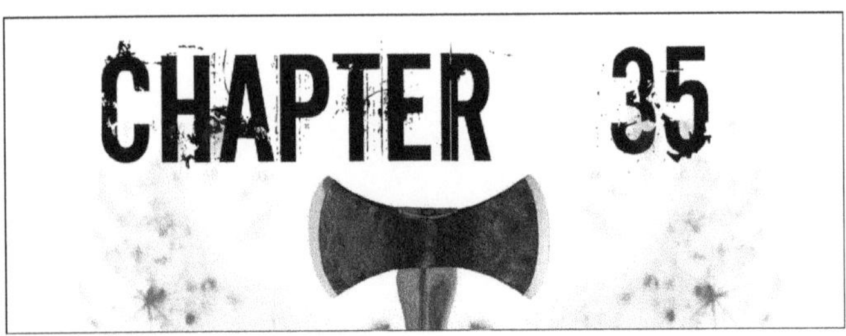

CHAPTER 35

The Tower of London dominated the skyline, silhouetted against the vacillating colors of the constant solar flares. Resolute it stood. A stubborn pile of stone and mortar that had survived countless regimes and wars. Both a bastion and a monument to human fortitude and perseverance.

In the street in front of the main gates stood a row of eight gibbets. Three of the gibbets were full. Two mature human males and one young female hung from them. Their tongues lolled from their slack jaws and their stomachs were distended with gas. Flies buzzed freely about them and ravens pecked at their exposed flesh.

Below each body lay a wooden plaque with the persons sentence scrawled across it in white paint. 'Sophistry.' 'Thievery.' 'Illegal Trading.'

A wave of anger rose in The Forever Man that was so strong he had to support himself against a wall. His breath came in short gasps and he had to quash his rage before it threatened to engulf him and cause him to lose his reason.

This was where the Fair-Folk said that Nathaniel should give himself up. No doubt he was to have been gibbeted for the public to see. An example of the Fair-Folk's supremacy over the humans.

He was also sure that this was where Milly would be imprisoned.

The Marine had arrived in London the day before and had been surprised at how many humans there were living there. He had spoken to a few, and common knowledge was that the bulk of the Fair-Folk in London lived either in the Tower or in the Palace of Westminster or in Buckingham Palace. All ancient buildings that had been built before the advent of central heating and electricity and modern flimsy materials. In point of fact, buildings that were built to last without the help of modern amenities or upkeep. Stone and hardwood as opposed to glass and plastic.

The bulk of the Orcs and goblins were barracked alongside the river in the many warehouses, docks, and churches.

Security surrounding the actual Tower of London was surprisingly lax, and human traders and servants seemed to enter and exit as and when they pleased. Nathaniel also noticed the odd member of the Fair-Folk leaving, ensconced in palanquins, curtains drawn so that only glimpses of them were possible.

Before he had done a recce of the area, Nathaniel had speculated over various ways to get into the Tower. These had ranged from the stealthy, climbing the walls under cover of darkness, to the ridiculous, disguising himself as a woman and gaining access by pretending to be a seamstress.

As it happened, he simply draped a piece of old sacking over his axe, waited for a large crowd of humans to enter the gates and then walked in with them, leaving ugly horse at a stables.

When he was inside he decided, once again, to stick with the simple and obvious rather than the complex and esoteric. So, he casually asked if anyone knew where the captured girl, Milly, was locked up.

The second person that he asked, a middle-aged woman, gave him directions to a room in the White Tower. She showed no interest in why he wanted to know and no curiosity as to who he was or why he was there. When he looked around him he noticed that most of the humans seemed similarly withdrawn and incurious. There was no smiling, no laughing. Voices were subdued and without emotion.

The whole place reminded him of documentaries that he had seen on East Germany before the wall went down.

There were two Orc guards at the foot of the stairway, but he simply nodded at them and walked on by, climbing the stairs at a slow and steady pace. As instructed, he turned left at the third floor and continued down the corridor. At the fourth door along stood an Orc guard.

Remembering how tough they were, Nathaniel garnered his power, walked up to the Orc, and simply hit him with a huge blow in the center of his chest.

All things considered, he overdid the amount of power that he used, and the Orc slammed through the door, smashing it off its hinges. He ended up, lying in the middle of the room, on top of the door, his armored chest plate stove in, barely breathing. Out for the count and more.

Milly turned from the window. 'Nathaniel. You came.'

'Of course,' said the Marine. 'What else?'

Milly smiled, her face a picture of radiance. 'You love me.' She ran over and threw her arms around him.

'Come on,' said Nathaniel. 'We've gotta move. Made a bit more noise than I wanted to. Didn't think that I'd actually knock old pig-face through the door.'

The Marine pulled Milly towards the door. But she resisted.

'Wait.'

'Why?' asked the Marine. 'We don't have time. Anything that you need we can pick up later. First, we need to get away from here. ASAP.'

'Stop, Nathaniel. We need to talk.'

'No time. Run first, talk later.'

'I'm not going,' said Milly.

Nathaniel stopped, his mouth hung open like a stranded goldfish. 'I don't understand. Not going where?'

'With you.'

'But you have to,' urged Nathaniel. 'And you have to right now before it's too late.'

Milly shook her head and smiled gently. 'No, Nathaniel. I don't have to. In fact … I want you to stay here. With me.'

The Marine shook his head.

'No, Nathaniel,' continued Milly. 'Wait. Listen. If you stay here we can be together. We can be the preeminent human couple in the country. We can help to govern our people. We can change things from within. No more bloodshed. No more threat of war. Of violence. Please, Nathaniel. Think about it.'

'Jesus, Milly,' said Nathaniel. 'Just outside in the street hang three humans. Three people put to death for nothing more than petty theft, selling something, and disagreeing with the Fair-Folk. You can't negotiate with these … alien things. Now come on.'

'Those people broke the law, Nathaniel. They knew the consequences. The Fair-Folk are hard but fair. And with you and I in charge of the human contingent, we can live a life of great worth. You can still be a king and I can be your queen.'

'King,' shouted Nathaniel. 'Do you think that I give a damn about being king? And king of what? Of who? King of the subjugated. King of the terrified and downtrodden. Gods, Milly, what the hell are you thinking?'

'I'm thinking of us,' screamed Milly. 'I don't care about the rest. I want us to be happy. To be together. I want to be queen.'

Nathaniel stared at the young woman for a while. And then his expression changed. His face hardened and any light of love or affection that may have been visible in his eyes was snuffed out.

'There is no, 'us,' Milly,' he said. 'There is only you and me.'

The Marine let go of her hand and walked towards the door, stopping, and turning to face her one last time before he left.

'Goodbye, Milly,' he said. 'Whatever I did, or didn't do, that turned you into … this … I apologize. Truly I do.'

The Marine walked back along the corridor and down the steps. Moving briskly but not running so as not to attract any unwanted attention.

Milly stood still for a while. She felt as though she had been gut shot. She had worked it all out. Nathaniel was meant to stay. Together they would be the king and queen of the humans. Feted and lauded over all. Treated by the Fair-Folk as almost-equals. No more living in fear. No more planning for war. No more constant life-and-death decisions.

But Nathaniel had rejected her again. And this time it had been worse than all of the other times. This time he had looked on her with an expression that could be described as nothing other than disgust.

Well never again.

She picked up her skirts and ran hard, tripling down the staircase and out into the yard. At full speed she ran around the base of the tower and headed to the training square where she knew that Orc Sergeant Kob spent most of every day sparring.

And, sure enough, there he was. She ran straight up to him.

'What are you doing out?' he asked. His tone more curious than threatening.

'He is here,' she said. Her voice a sharp whisper, as if imparting information too important or simply too incendiary for all to hear.

'Who?'

'Him. The Forever Man.'

She waited, expecting questions. Denials. A need for proof. But Kob was unlike other Orcs and he simply looked at her for a few seconds while he assimilated the information.

'When did he leave?'

'Less than a minute ago. Not sure which way he went. Find him,' she continued. 'He is an enemy of the people. Bring him back to face retribution.'

Kob did not answer. He simply sheathed his broadsword and strode off. Heading towards the gates.

'Must I tell anyone else?' shouted Milly after him.

He turned to face her. 'No,' he shook his head. 'I will take care of it. Go back to your room immediately, before you get in to trouble.'

And then he was gone.

***

Sergeant Kob ran hard. He had not lied to the human Milly. He did not actually say that he would tell others about The Forever Man, he had simply said that he would take care of things. And he would. He was going to chase him down and bring him back for justice.

Ever since he had first come across The Forever Man and had been beaten in single combat by him, he had become obsessed. No one else could even come close to defeating him but the thin-skin had beaten him with relative ease. And then he had spared his life, swinging his battle-axe at Kob's neck, and then stopping as the blade touched the skin. An acknowledgement of his skill. Proof that he could have killed if he had wanted to.

So Kob had trained relentlessly. Driving himself beyond what a normal mortal being normally would. Working his strength, his speed, his battle-consciousness. Now he finally had a chance for a rematch and he didn't want any other Orcs or goblins getting in the way.

This time he would win. No one could stand against him. He was simply too fast, too strong, and just too damn good at what he did.

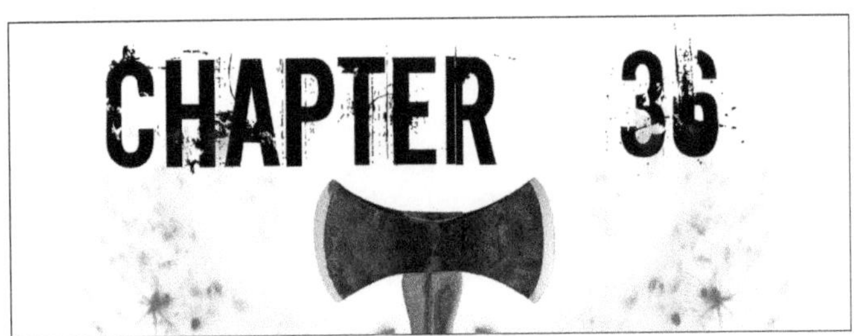

CHAPTER 36

Nathaniel knew that he was being followed. He just wasn't sure what, or whom, the potential assailant was. It was nothing as overt as an actual sighting. It was more of a feeling. A sense of being followed. Every now and then he would stop and look behind him. Sometimes, in the distance, he would see the hint of a shadow that shouldn't be there. Or a shivering tree branch. Perhaps a tiny feather of condensation in the air.

Whatever, or whoever it was, thought Nathaniel, it was quick. Because the Marine had been riding ugly horse hard, pushing it to its limits for almost two days and the follower was still there and he had seen no signs of another horse.

He had tried using his power to identify the follower, but it was no use. He simply didn't have the finesse necessary. All that he could deem was that there was someone and that was all.

So that morning, before sunrise, he led his horse into a long narrow vale that ran through the forest. He tethered ugly horse back under cover of thick foliage and waited, his mouth and nose covered in a strip of material to stop his breath fogging. Still. Patient.

After forty minutes his vigil was rewarded as an Orc came into view. But Nathaniel could tell straight away that it was no normal Orc. The creature moved with great stealth and great speed. Almost graceful.

'I know you,' whispered the Marine to himself. 'Should have killed you when I had the chance,' he continued scanning for more pursuers, but after a couple of minutes, saw none. 'Odd,' he said to himself as he slipped back to his horse and led it quietly away. 'Why is he alone?'

The Marine pushed hard all day and then, at sundown, he stopped for a short break and grabbed a bite to eat. Hard bread and cheese, and then he continued. His plan was to keep going all night and give the Orc the slip. He remembered well the last time that they had met, and although he was sure that he could take him in battle, he saw no reason to deliberately court danger.

The next morning, as the sun rose, Nathaniel lay in watch once again.

To his amazement, the Orc was still on his tail. And he was chasing on foot.

The Marine smiled and stood up, no longer bothering with concealment. He went to ugly horse, took a small pack of hard bread, a slice of cheese, and a handful of dried fruit from his saddle bag, put them into a pouch and tied it to his waist. Then he slung a full water bottle over his shoulder and made sure that his axe was settled in his belt.

'Okay, ugly horse,' he said to his mount. 'We're not that far from home. Do you know the way?'

The horse stared at him. Expressionless.

Nathaniel smacked it on its rump. 'Go home, boy,' he shouted. Ugly stared at him for a while longer and then turned and trotted off, heading in the correct direction.

Nathaniel waited until the horse was out of sight and then he turned to face the distant Orc.

'Hey!' He waved his hands in the air. 'No horse. Just you and me.'

The Orc stopped running, looked at the Marine and answered his wave.

'Right,' said Nathaniel as he turned towards home. 'Let's see just how tough you are.'

And he started to run.

***

Kob had been chasing the thin-skin, Nathaniel, for three days now and he was bone-tired. Keeping up with another biped was one thing but trying to outrun a horse was another thing entirely. Kob had tried to ride before but try as he might, a horse would go insane whenever he, or any other Orc went near it.

They had no idea why. So, when it came to transport it was Shanks's Pony all the way.

He had suspected that the human knew that he was being followed but he had been taken by complete surprise when, this morning at first light, the thin-skin had stood up, waved to get his attention, and then shown him that he was no longer going to ride his horse, thereby leveling the playing fields.

Sergeant Kob already had a vast amount of respect for this human as he was the only being to have ever bested him in single combat and now, with the thin skin's latest demonstration, he felt even more admiration for him.

As a rule, Orcs did not have friends. Nor did they have partners. But if Kob had ever entertained the concept of friendship, then he was sure that this strange human would be an entity well worthy of his comradeship.

He adjusted his broadsword on his back, took a swig of water from his flask and started to run. Long, loping strides that he could keep going all day and night if necessary.

***

Nathaniel ran along the game trail, not bothering about the clear tracks that he was leaving behind him. The Orc was obviously too skilled at tracking to be put off by anything as blatant as sweeping the trail or darting off into the underbrush.

But, as he ran, the Marine was formulating a plan. He was simply waiting for the right moment to execute it.

Soon he saw a good spot up ahead. He immediately left the trail at a right angle, running off into the undergrowth for about twenty yards and then, mid-stride, he stopped, and slowly and very carefully, he backtracked. Stepping in his own footsteps so it appeared as though he had been running and simply disappeared.

When he arrived back at the point where he had deviated from the trail, he ran on for thirty yards or so, preparing himself as he did.

And, as he passed under a tree branch that was sticking out over the track, some twelve feet in the air, he launched himself up with a mighty jump and grabbed it, fingers scrabbling desperately at the icy coating. Then, moving with care and stealth, he climbed along the branch and then jumped to the next tree. Once again, his trail had simply stopped as if he had flown away.

He kept moving from tree to tree until the gap between the trees was too great and he then climbed back down to ground level and set off running once again.

'Ha,' he said to himself. 'Work that one out, Mister Orc. I think not.'

***

As Sergeant Kob ran he wondered at what he had done. Why had he chased after the thin-skin without telling his commander that he was doing so? Why had he left, unaided by any other Orcs or goblins? Why hadn't he shouted the alarm when the human Milly had told him of The Forever Mans presence?

He could not think of a viable answer. He might say that a single warrior could travel faster by himself. He might argue that a lone tracker could remain unseen for longer than a contingent. But he knew, in his heart of hearts, that these arguments were specious. And, as a result, he also knew that, whatever the outcome, when he returned back to his garrison, his Fair-Folk leaders would punish him. It would be a short rope and a long drop for him. As it should be, he agreed to himself as he ran. He had acted irresponsibly and recklessly and had disobeyed protocol.

And all because of his own vanity. A trait that the pod-bred Orcs were not even meant to possess. He wanted to test himself against the thin-skin. He wanted to fight him again to see if the last time had been mere bad luck or simple circumstance.

If he managed to beat The Forever Man then he would return home and face his punishment. It would have been worth it. If he lost … well … he laughed to himself, there would be nothing to worry about as his head would most definitely be well separated from his body, courtesy of the huge axe that the thin-skin used so well.

He turned a corner on the game track and saw, immediately, that the human's tracks split. One set carried on straight and another veered off sharply to the right, plunging into the thick undergrowth.

Kob stopped running and thought. What he saw in front of him was obviously not possible. A man could not be traveling in two directions at the same time. He decided to follow the tracks that veered off into the undergrowth. He moved quickly and silently, sacrificing speed for stealth. But after twenty yards the tracks simply disappeared. He cast about, running on for another twenty yards and then circling the vanishing point. Nothing.

He squatted down on his haunches and thought for a while. Could The Forever Man fly? The Orc shrugged to himself. Who knows? Maybe he could. But Kob assumed that, a man such as The Forever Man would not use his gift of flight in this situation. He reckoned that he would see it as … unfair.

Kob stood up and ran back to the track, to follow the set of prints that had continued on straight. After thirty yards or so—they too disappeared.

The Orc sergeant took a deep breath, sat down in the snow, and pulled out a stick of jerked beef to gnaw on and he thought.

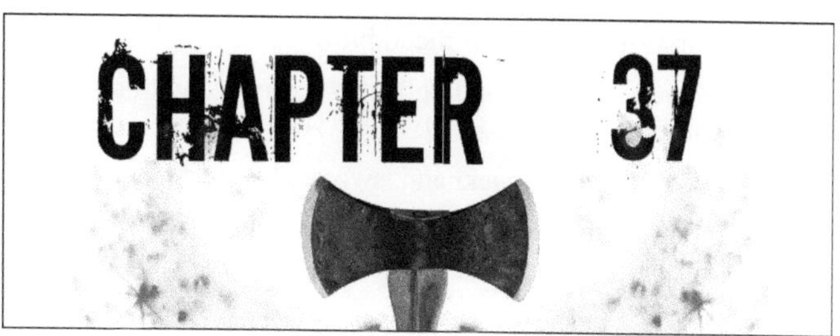

Nathaniel had a small, smokeless fire going and he sat close, toasting a piece of hard bread on a stick. Turning it constantly to stop it burning. After a few more seconds he pulled it from the flames and took an experimental bite. It was warm but still rock hard and stale, but he chewed and swallowed nonetheless. Eating to replenish energy.

'Come,' he said. 'Sit by the fire. It's small but warm. Warmer than no fire, at least.'

Orc Sergeant Kob walked up to the fire and squatted opposite the Marine.

'You used the trees,' said Kob. 'Swung from branch to branch. Took me two hours to find your spoor again.'

Nathaniel laughed. 'Pretty clever, hey?'

Kob nodded. 'But then you squandered your lead to make a fire and toast some old bread. Why?'

The Marine shrugged. 'I think that you probably would have caught up with me before the wall. You're fast. I mean, I am faster, but I suspect that you have the lead on me when it comes to stamina. I burn hot but fast. Better sprinter than long distance runner. So, I figured, if it's a fight that you're looking for, now is as good a time as any.'

'True,' agreed the Orc. 'So, what now?'

Nathaniel stood up and stretched. 'Now, we fight.'

'Armed or unarmed?' enquired Sergeant Kob.

'Oh, armed,' said Nathaniel. 'This isn't some sort of fight club. This is for real.' He unclipped his battle-axe from his belt and Kob drew his massive broadsword.

Kob swung first. A massive overhand blow.

Nathaniel swayed to his left and deflected the sword with his own blade and then he countered with a backhand.

The Orc ducked under the backhand, swiveled, and struck again.

As the fight progressed the two contestants sped up. Metal crashed against metal. Sparks flew, and steam boiled off both warriors as they clashed again and again.

Neither drew blood and neither could gain the upper hand.

There was no finesse in the way that they fought. It was all about speed, strength, and endurance. Every blow was a massive, killing swing. Every parry was a desperate hack. The very forest itself shuddered at the colossal onslaught.

And then The Forever Man realized, with a heavy heart, that he was actually holding back. He was deliberately slowing his reaction time down by microseconds. Not much, but just enough to allow the Orc to stay in the battle. Enough to allow the creature to retain some semblance of honor.

Kob faked a blow to Nathaniel's head and then he jumped back and grounded his sword.

He held his hand up. 'Wait,' he said. 'What are you doing?'

'Fighting,' answered Nathaniel. 'What else?'

Kob shook his head. 'You could have blooded me many times already, but you haven't. Why?'

Nathaniel shrugged.

'Please,' continued Kob. 'You do me no honor in holding back. I beg you, give me your all. There is no dishonor in losing to a warrior such as you.' The Orc sergeant raised his sword up again, took a deep breath and lunged towards the Marine.

The Forever Man exploded, smashing the Orc's sword aside and kicking him in the chest, forcing him back and up the hill that they were fighting on.

Kob fought with renewed effort, spinning, and ducking, and lashing out with his steel. But his efforts were for aught. The Forever man was as the wind before him. Powerful, unstoppable, and untouchable as his double-bladed axe blocked Kob's massive blows, turning them aside with consummate ease as he smashed open his armor, hammering it to pieces, blow by blow.

Kob retreated, stumbling backwards and further up the hill as the demigod of war hacked and slashed and cut. Blood flowed freely from the Orcs forehead and chest and arm but none of the blows was enough to dismember or kill, and Kob could sense that, even now, The Forever Man was not fighting at close to his full potential.

Finally, when they got to the top of the small hill that they had been battling on, Kob succumbed to his exhaustion and fell to his knees, his sword held limply in his hand with no strength left to lift it, let alone wield it in combat.

He smiled to himself. It had been a good fight. There was no shame in losing to this magnificent being that had bested him with apparent ease. No shame at all.

He looked up at The Forever Man who stood above him. Not a cut nor mark upon his face nor body. Not a bead of sweat. Not even a rip in his clothes to betray the fact that he had just fought the ultimate Orc warrior to a standstill.

Kob rested his head on his chest and waited for the blade that would end his life. He knew that the cut would be strong and sure, and his death would be clean. There would be no rope for him. No ignominious death by the hand of his so-called superiors. For him would be the true honor of the warriors' death. A death by the blade.

He waited.

But nothing came.

He looked up at the Forever Man and saw that the human was staring at something. Over Kob's head. Looking at something in the valley below him.

Kob turned to see what Nathaniel was staring at.

The entire valley was packed with rank upon rank of brightly armored creatures. And the air above was full of flying versions of the same thing.

'What are they?' he asked.

'Annihilators,' answered The Forever Man as he held out his hand to help Kob to his feet.

The two of them stared at the mass of living beings below them.

'The Vandals told me that they were coming,' said Nathaniel. 'I didn't take them seriously enough.' He turned to face the Orc sergeant. 'Listen, my new friend, we have a problem. These things are bad. Worse than you and I put together. And I tell you something for nothing—they are here to destroy us all. Humans, Fair-Folk, goblins, and Orcs.'

'I believe you,' said Kob. 'With your leave I will return home as swiftly as possible and warn our leaders.'

'As will I,' said Nathaniel

The two unlikely allies shook hands, forearm to forearm as warriors do.

'My friends call me Nathaniel,' said the Marine.

'I have no friends,' retorted the Orc.

'You do now,' said Nathaniel. 'So, what do I call you?'

The Orc tilted his head to one side as he thought about the concept of friendship. 'You can call me Kob.' Then he picked up his sword, slid it into his scabbard and started to run for home.

Just before he entered the forest he turned to face the Marine and he waved. 'Thank you, friend.'

And then he was gone.

Nathaniel clipped his axe to his belt, gave the massed Enemy one last look and then headed for the wall and his people.

Once again, The Forever Man was preparing for war.

Lightning Source UK Ltd.
Milton Keynes UK
UKHW040152111221
395376UK00003BA/621